TRUE
HORROR
STORIES

TRUE
HORROR
STORIES

TERRANCE DICKS

Robinson Children's Books

Robinson Publishing Ltd
7 Kensington Church Court
London W8 4SP

First published in the UK by Robinson Children's
Books, an imprint of Robinson Publishing Ltd 1997

A copy of the British Library Cataloguing in
Publications data is available from the British Library.

ISBN 1 85487 457 8

Printed and bound in the UK

1 3 5 7 9 10 8 6 4 2

Contents

INTRODUCTION

WHAT'S YOUR IDEA OF TRUE HORROR?

Clinging to a lifebelt in tropical seas, as circling sharks move ever closer? Feeling the deadly funnel-web spider crawling up your leg? Finding yourself the helpless captive of ruthless terrorists – or the victim of a blood-crazed killer? Is it the supernatural? Objects flying through the air in a haunted house, mysterious apparitions, the howl of the werewolf, the fangs of the vampire?

Or is it the alien and the unknown? Do you worry about strange lights in the sky, UFOs, flying saucers filled with little green men who might swoop down, carry you away, and use you for unpleasant medical experiments?

Is it fire? Being trapped in a blazing inferno, at sea, in the Australian bush or on city streets? It's a dangerous world out there.

Here's a round-up of horrors, a whole series of true and terrifying events. Read about them and shudder – but don't get too upset. After all, nothing like this could ever happen to you.

COULD IT?

C H A P T E R 1
SOME GHASTLY GHOSTS

The Pointless Poltergeist

One of the commonest kind of ghost, reported throughout the ages and all over the world, is the poltergeist – a German word meaning "noisy ghost". The odd thing about poltergeists is they all operate in very much the same way. Poltergeists are the hooligans of the supernatural world, specializing in stupid, destructive and sometimes dangerous tricks. They make sinister sounds, they slam doors, they chuck furniture about, and smash crockery. Just like your average teenager in a temper, really. . .

The earliest recorded poltergeist appeared at a place called Bingen in Germany in AD 858. For some reason it had a grudge against a local farmer. It started off by throwing stones at his farmhouse, went on to cause mysterious fires, and even developed a ghostly voice, following the farmer around and shouting about his sins. It even accused him of seducing one of his servant girls. All very embarrassing. . .

The Demon Drummer

In England, in 1661, a poltergeist began persecuting a magistrate. There's a very full account in an imposingly titled book – *Saducismus Triumphatis: or Full and Plain Evidence con-*

cerning Witches and Apparitions. Written by the Reverend Joseph Glanville, it was published in 1666, five years after the mysterious events it recounts. One day the magistrate, who was called John Mompesson, was in the little country town of Ludgarshal visiting the bailiff when he heard a loud drumming in the street outside.

Asked about the row, the bailiff told him that the town was being troubled by a wandering drummer, a sort of seventeenth-century busker. Not only did the man go round constantly banging his drum, he'd been trying to get money out of the local constable with the backing of some kind of official papers.

Mompesson had the man hauled out of the local ale-house and brought before him. The drummer, who was called John Drury, said defiantly that he had a "warrant" for his drumming and was entitled to a cash grant as well, and to support his claim he then produced his papers.

The magistrate examined the documents and decided that they were forged. He took away the man's drum and ordered the constable to lock him up. The drummer broke down, confessed the forgeries and pleaded for the return of his drum. Mompesson wouldn't listen.

The case disposed of – or so he thought – Mompesson went home to nearby Tedworth, leaving the drummer locked up and, his drum with the bailiff.

The drummer pleaded with the constable to let him go. Eventually the constable agreed. The drummer asked for his drum back, but the bailiff wouldn't give it to him, and so Drury left without it. Not knowing what to do with the drum, the bailiff sent it to Mompesson's house.

Soon after the drum arrived at his house, Mompesson had to make a trip to London. When he got back his terrified wife told him there'd been mysterious noises in the night while he was away.

A few nights later the trouble started again. The magistrate was woken up by a loud banging, first on the front door and then on the wooden walls of the house. Grabbing a pair of pistols, Mompesson dashed out to deal with the intruder – but there was no one to be seen. When he went back to bed he heard a strange, hollow drumming sound coming from the roof. Eventually it faded away.

A few nights later, the mysterious drumming returned. It continued for five nights, stopped for three, then started up again for another five. The disturbances continued, keeping to the same pattern.

Before long the noises moved into the house,

The Demon Drummer

centring on the room where the drum was kept. The hollow booming seemed to come from all over the house. It went into the bedrooms, where the deep throbbing rattled windows and shook beds. The entire family was terrified, and so were all the servants. No one was getting any sleep.

The ghostly drummer began to imitate horses' hooves, and the rattling of peas into a pot. It played military tattoos and made scratching sounds under beds. As is often the case with poltergeists, it attached itself to the children, following them about the house. It threw ashes into their beds and emptied their chamber-pots into them. After terrifying a servant, "It left in that roome a sulphureous smell which was very offensive" – perhaps the first example in psychic history of a farting ghost. At night it would frighten the Mompesson children, shaking their beds so hard it seemed they would fall to pieces. It would lift the beds up and then slam them down again. It made mysterious scratching and scuttling sounds, howled like a cat and panted like a dog. Sometimes it would tug at the children's nightgowns and pull their hair. Family prayers kept the poltergeist temporarily quiet – but as soon as prayers were over "The chairs walkt about the room of themselves, the Children's shoes were hurled over their heads and every loose thing moved about the chamber."

Once it alarmed everyone by shouting "A

witch! A witch!" from an empty room. It snatched off the servants' bedclothes and threw their shoes at their heads. It produced blue and shimmering lights that came down the chimney and gave people sore eyes. It put a pike into Mompesson's bed, and an upright knife into his mother's. Weirdest of all, John Mompesson went into his stables one morning and found his favourite horse lying on its back with one of its hind legs jammed into its mouth!

Mompesson tried everything. Well-meaning friends came to investigate. They all heard the strange sounds, and saw the shaking beds and the flying furniture, but could do nothing to help. The prayers of the local priest didn't seem to make any difference. Mompesson persuaded the King to send two court officials, Lord Falmouth and Lord Chesterfield, to observe the phenomenon. Rather unsportingly, the poltergeist refused to perform while they were there. As soon as they left, it started up again.

Mompesson felt sure that John Drury, the man he'd arrested in Ludgarshal, had something to do with his troubles. He set about trying to trace him, prepared to threaten the man with prosecution. To his astonishment he discovered that John Drury was already in Gloucester jail. Deprived of his drum, and his dodgy documents, Drury had turned to more straightforward crime. He had been arrested for stealing pigs. Asked if he knew anything about the weird events at Mompesson's house, John Drury readily admitted responsibility. "I have plagued him and he shall never be at quiet, till he hath made me satisfaction for taking away my drum." Drury also boasted of being in possession of certain "Gallant books he had of an odd fellow, who was counted a Wizzard".

As a result of these rash confessions, John Drury was charged not only with pig-stealing but with witchcraft as well. In the event he was narrowly acquitted of witchcraft, but convicted of being a rogue and a vagabond and sentenced to be transported.

Soon afterwards, the mysterious happenings at John Mompesson's house stopped as suddenly as they had begun.

At least for a time. Then the ghostly drums, and all the other mysterious events, started up again. Apparently the fiendish John Drury had escaped from the convict ship by "affrighting the sailors and conjuring up a storm", and was back in England...

Luckily for poor Mompesson's sanity, the mysterious manifestations soon came to a stop, this time for good. There's no record of John Drury's final fate. Perhaps he was captured and transported again – or even executed. Perhaps he decided that the loss of his drum was avenged.

Although it's rare for a poltergeist to be so directly under someone's control, in many respects the Drummer of Tedworth is a classic poltergeist, with an extraordinary number of weird and freakish effects. Especially since children were involved. (More about this later.)

The Cock Lane Ghost

Poltergeists continued to be reported throughout the ages. In 1762 the Cock Lane Ghost had all London in an uproar.

One night in 1756, a woman called Fanny Kent was left alone in her lodgings in Cock Lane, Smithfield. Her husband, the clerk of the local church, was away for the night, attending a wedding in the country.

Afraid of sleeping alone, Fanny asked if her landlord's eleven year-old daughter Elizabeth would spend the night with her. Mr Parsons, the landlord, agreed and the two went to bed. That night Fanny and Elizabeth were disturbed by strange bumps, rappings and scratchings, on the bedposts, under the bed, and from various parts of the room.

Fanny was terrified. When her husband returned, she told him she was sure the strange events meant she was going to die. And die she did, though not until some time later, apparently from smallpox.

Eighteen months after Fanny's death, the mysterious noises started again, this time centred around the bed of the child, Elizabeth Parsons. There were so many mysterious thumps and bangs that Mr Parsons ripped out the wainscoting around Elizabeth's bed, just to make sure no one was playing tricks.

Elizabeth's nurse, a girl called Mary Frazer, worked out a way of communicating with the ghost. One knock for "Yes", two knocks for "No" – a method used in hundreds of ghost investigations in later years.

By question and answer, Mary Frazer discovered that the ghost was that of Fanny Kent. Fanny said her husband had poisoned her by putting arsenic in her beer and she wanted to see him hanged. The story of this ghostly accusation soon got out, and Mr Kent had a very uncomfortable time. People started pointing him out in the street.

The ghost's fame grew and all sorts of important and fashionable people turned up to see, or rather hear, it. They included the Duke of York, the writer Horace Walpole, the Bishop of Salisbury, and many others.

The poet Oliver Goldsmith even wrote a pamphlet about it, called *The Mystery Revealed*. In it he described a typical "seance" as they were later to be called. During this scene, Elizabeth was tucked up in bed and the ghost-hunters trooped in. Goldsmith explains that they had to behave in a quiet, respectful manner. "For if they show

Dr Samuel Johnson investigates

either before, or when the knocking is begun, a too prying, inquisitive or ludicrous turn of thinking, the ghost continues usually silent or, to use the expression of the house, Miss Fanny is angry." If all went well, the ghost announced itself by scratching. It would then answer questions by the "one knock for yes, two for no" method.

The Cock Lane ghost became so famous that more official tests were arranged. One of them was attended by Dr Samuel Johnson, the most famous literary figure of the day. The Doctor a stern rationalist, wasn't much impressed by the ghost. It was decided, "in the opinion of the whole assembly," as he later wrote, "that the child has some art of making or counterfeiting particular noises, and that there is no agency of any higher cause."

Elizabeth was subjected to further tests. In two of them she was strung up in a hammock. This time the ghost didn't appear. Elizabeth was threatened with prison, for herself and her father. On the next test she was caught with a small board and a piece of wood under her dress. Sceptics said this proved the ghost was a fake all along.

Elizabeth's supporters said indignantly that the child had simply been frightened into cheating. They also pointed out that the feeble noises she managed to fake were nothing like the noises so many people had heard earlier.

The authorities weren't convinced. Mr Parsons, Elizabeth's father, and Mary Frazer, her nurse, were put on trial with several others, and convicted of conspiracy against the life of Mr Kent, Fanny's unfortunate husband.

Mr Parsons was sentenced to the pillory, a common punishment of the time. But the public weren't convinced of his guilt. They preferred to believe in the ghost. When Parsons appeared in the pillory, they pelted him not with the usual dead cats and rubbish, but with money!

One can't help suspecting that Mr Parsons had managed to turn the family ghost into a nice little earner. The ghost-hunting visitors Oliver Goldsmith describes were no doubt paying for the privilege. However, there is something curiously convincing in the theory that Elizabeth only cheated because she was scared by the threat of imprisonment.

The story of the Cock Lane Ghost survives because such famous writers as Oliver Goldsmith and Samuel Johnson took an interest. No poltergeist ever had a more impressive literary pedigree.

Borley Rectory

If poltergeists, and other ghosts, were to have a home from home, then the ideal place would have been Borley Rectory in Essex, often described as "the most haunted house in England".

The rambling red-brick building was first built in 1863 by the Reverend Henry Bull. It's believed that an old monastery originally stood on the same site. The Rectory was enlarged in 1875 to accommodate the Reverend's ever-increasing family – he had seventeen children!

Since then the Rectory changed hands several times, and considering what went on there, it's hardly surprising – Borley Rectory's ghosts were anything but reticent. There are hundreds of accounts of the Borley hauntings. A new maid heard dragging footsteps going past her door at night and she was so terrified she soon gave in her notice.

The same steps were also heard by one of the Reverend Bull's daughters and another daughter was awakened by mysterious raps on her door, and by an invisible something slapping her face.

A visitor of the same period reported stones flying about, and books and clothes hurled around her room. One night all the bells in the house – twenty of them – started ringing at once. Then there was a sound of rushing water. At night a ghostly coach-and-four was often heard rumbling past the house. Even in the gardener's cottage there were mysterious crashing sounds, and the padding footsteps of a ghostly dog.

In 1929 Harry Price, a well-known psychic investigator of the time, visited Borley Rectory on behalf of a newspaper. As Price entered the house to keep a night-time vigil, a half-brick whizzed past his head, shattering a french window. Inside the house, a red-glass candle-stick flew through the air, shattering on the iron stove in the hall. Pebbles and bits of slate came flying down the stairs. Bells rang for no reason and keys jumped out of locks. In a bed-room a cake of soap flew from a washstand with terrific force, hitting a china jug.

That night Harry Price and two of the Bull daughters held a seance. They made contact with a rapping ghost. Communicating with them by the usual one tap "yes", two taps "no" method, it claimed to be the spirit of the late Reverend Bull himself.

In 1930 a new vicar moved into the Rectory. He kept a careful and detailed diary, recording hundreds of weird events. This diary tells us that jugs and other bits of crockery vanished and reappeared; There was a strange smell of lavender – and a lavender bag kept appearing, vanishing, then reappearing; cotton reels, a hairbrush and a broken hammer were hurled across a bedroom. The vicar also recorded that stones and other small missiles were hurled all the time, sometimes twelve or thirteen in one night.

By 1937 the Rectory, not surprisingly, was vacant again. Seeing a great ghost-hunting opportunity, Harry Price rented it for a year. He advertised for voluntary ghostbusters, and assembled a team of over forty volunteers, though they were not psychic investigators as such, but doctors, army officers and lawyers.

The volunteers took it in turn to stay at the Rectory. All of them reported strange noises, flying objects, things vanishing and reappearing and weird markings on the walls. One of them made contact with a spirit who threatened to burn the Rectory down. At the end of the year, Harry Price had enough material for a book, *The Most Haunted House in England*. Later, he published a sequel – *The End of Borley Rectory*.

Harry Price was later accused of exaggerating, or even inventing, the strange happenings, but it's hard to explain away Borley Rectory's long and spooky history. Besides innumerable hurled objects of every kind, a wide variety of tapping, rapping, scratching and scuttling sounds, bell-ringing and ghostly foot-steps, and the constant vanishing and reap-pearing of bits of domestic equipment, there had been many other strange manifestations at Borley over the years.

These include a ghostly nun, a headless man, and a woman in white. Messages asking for help have appeared on walls or on scraps of paper. Strange voices and wailing sounds were heard time and time again.

In 1935 the Church decided, not surprisingly, that the place wasn't suitable for a Rectory. In 1939 the building was extensively damaged in a mysterious fire, after which it had become more or less a ruin.

 Perhaps the resident ghosts became tired of the constant stream of vicars, visitors, exorcists and investigators, and decided they'd like the place to themselves.

The Electric Ghost

If you want a more modern poltergeist, there's the affair of the haunted office. It happened in 1967, in Rosenheim, Germany. In this haunted office neon lights failed, photocopiers leaked fluids, light bulbs exploded and mysterious rappings came from the walls. And if these happenings weren't sufficiently spooky, there were paintings which spun on the walls, file drawers which opened and closed, and a heavy metal filing-cabinet which moved about by itself.

The lawyer who occupied the office got a huge telephone bill showing hundreds of calls to the speaking clock service. He had all the office phones cut off except his own, which he kept under constant watch. The mystery calls continued. In order to establish the cause of the disturbances, the power company installed special monitoring equipment and discovered enormous power fluctuations at the same time as the strange events.

At this point, a team of psychic investigators were called in. They found that the disturbances had started with the arrival of a new employee, a nineteen-year-old girl. When the phenomena occurred, the girl suffered a sort of hysterical paralysis. Interestingly, when the girl left and went to work in another office, the mysterious events came to an end.

Possession

Similar to poltergeist activity, but very much more sinister, is the phenomenon called demonic possession. As with poltergeists, there are numerous examples throughout the ages. There's even a passage in the Bible (Mark 9: 17-27) relating how Jesus cast out an evil spirit. In this story, the young man had been afflicted for many years. According to his father, the spirit had often thrown him into fire and water in an attempt to destroy him. When the victim was brought to him, convulsing and foaming at the mouth, Jesus ordered the evil spirit to depart. "Leave him, I command you, and never enter him again."

Out the spirit came, shrieking aloud, and the young man collapsed as if dead. Jesus raised him up, and he recovered.

St Norbert and the Devil

There's an account from medieval times of St Norbert struggling with a demon who had possessed a little girl. At first the demon defied him. "Not for thee or for any other will I come forth!" So St Norbert had the possessed girl brought to the altar of his church and read passages from the Bible to her. The demon just roared with evil laughter. When the Saint held up the sacred Host it cried, "See how he holds the little god in his hands!" The angry Saint then prayed at the demon so long and so hard that it screamed, "I burn, I burn! I am dying! I am dying!" Finally it howled "I will go forth!" and departed – "leaving behind a trail of unspeakably stinking urine." The girl was taken home, where she recovered. The Saint presumably sent for a medieval mop and bucket.

The Devils of Loudon

One of the most spectacular instances of possession took place in 1633 at the convent in the small French town of Loudon. Suddenly lots of the inmates started carrying on in a most un-nun-like way, writhing about half-naked, screaming blasphemies and obscenities, and making extremely improper suggestions to shocked male visitors. The scandalized Church authorities investigated, and eventually charged Urbain Grandier, the local parish priest, with bewitching the nuns and causing them to be possessed with demons. The ecclesiastical investigators claimed to have found "devil marks" on his body. Grandier was arrested and savagely tortured, but he refused to confess. He was found guilty, and burned at the stake.

Grandier's death didn't put an end to the troubles. Cases of possession continued amongst the nuns of Loudon for many years. Stranger still, several of the priests who had conducted Grandier's interrogation seemed to become possessed themselves. One became delirious and died, another went mad.

The famous novelist Aldous Huxley used the disturbing events at Loudon as a basis for his novel, *The Devils of Loudon*.

Years later, film director Ken Russell made it the subject of a highly lurid film, *The Devils*, filling the screen with bleeding bodies and naked nuns.

Demons Today

A famous modern case of demonic possession occurred in America in Mount Rainier, Washington State. A thirteen-year old boy called Douglass Deen was attacked by poltergeist-like phenomena.

It began quietly enough with mysterious scratching sounds. Douglass's parents suspected an insect invasion and sent for the exterminators, but nothing was found. Next came the familiar poltergeist trick of flying objects.

The Exorcism

Dishes and fruit flew through the air, and pictures jumped off the walls. Then the spirit turned its attention to Douglass himself. Whenever he went to bed, the bed itself started to shudder and vibrate.

Things got so bad that the Deens called in their local priest. He and Douglass settled down to spend the night in a room with twin beds. Before long the scratching sounds returned, and Douglass's bed started to shudder and vibrate. The priest fixed up a temporary bed in an armchair and got Douglass to sleep in that. It vibrated just as badly. A bed on the floor reacted in just the same way.

Douglass was taken to hospital for medical and psychiatric treatment. Nothing much seemed to be wrong with him, either mentally or physically, and none of the treatments helped. The strange psychic phenomena, the scratching and the shuddering, vibrating bed, continued even in hospital.

Eventually exorcism – the old church ceremony for casting out devils – was tried as a last resort. Two Jesuit priests performed the ceremony. Douglass reacted violently, shouting obscenities and screaming in Latin – a language he didn't know. After no less than thirty attempts, the cleansing ceremony appeared to work and the invading spirit faded away.

The affair is said to be one of the inspirations for William Peter Blatty's novel *The Exorcist*, published in 1971. In the book the possessed victim is a little girl. The book, a first-class supernatural chiller, aroused new interest in demonic possession, and in the Church's ancient remedy – exorcism. With great reluctance, Church authorities admitted that the service of exorcism still formed part of its religious armoury – and was still in use, even in modern times.

Blatty's book became a best-seller. It was later made into a successful film. Anyone who's seen it on late-night TV will remember the deep shuddering voice of the demon, the little girl's rotating head – and some very impressive projectile vomiting . . .

Horror at Amityville

Another terrifying instance of poltergeist-like activity also occurred in America. It took place in the peaceful little town of Amityville, on Long Island. This time it was not a person but a house that seemed possessed by an evil spirit.

It began when the Lutz family – George and Kathleen Lutz and their three children – bought a new house. The house was a beautiful three-storied colonial mansion, and it was going cheap – for a very good reason. It had once been the scene of a multiple murder:

In 1974 a young man called Ronald Defoe wiped out his entire family. After drugging them at dinner, he shot his parents and all his brothers and sisters with a rifle. Convicted of the crime, Ronald Defoe was sentenced to life imprisonment. His only defence was that a

The House at Amityville

mysterious "voice" had ordered him to commit the crimes.

A house with a horrible history like this isn't too easy to sell. It had to be put on the market at a very low price. Since the house was such a bargain, and it was exactly what he wanted, George Lutz bought the place and the family moved in. As they were aware of the house's sinister history, they decided to take no chances. They called in the local priest to bless their new home.

Trouble started the moment the priest began the ceremony. When he sprinkled the holy water a deep voice boomed, "Get out!" For the next two nights the Lutzes were awakened by strange noises. On the third night there was a splintering crash. George Lutz ran downstairs to investigate – and found that the heavy front door had been wrenched open, and was hanging from one steel hinge. The twisted metal and the position of the door made it clear that it had been smashed open by some terrific force from *inside* the house.

It was just the beginning. According to George Lutz, the house seemed to take on an evil life of its own. Windows and doors opened and closed of their own accord. Banisters were wrenched from the staircase and hurled downstairs. Worst of all, George Lutz awoke one night and found his wife Kathleen floating high above the bed. He managed to pull her down by her hair – and saw, to his horror, that her face was hideously distorted.

Kathleen screamed when she saw herself in the mirror. "It's not me, it's not me!" she cried. It was hours before her twisted features returned to normal.

A few nights later George and Kathleen were together in the sitting room when they saw red eyes glaring at them from the darkness outside. They rushed outside, but there was no one there. They saw footprints on the snowy ground – made by a cloven hoof.

The Lutz family just couldn't take any more. They decided to leave – after only twenty-eight days in their new home. Even as they packed, strange noises filled the air and green slime started oozing from the walls . . .

The events at Amityville gave rise to a book and two films. Jay Anson's best-selling book, *The Amityville Horror* was based on George Lutz's account of his terrifying experiences in the house. The book was later filmed, but the movie-makers didn't take any chances. Rather than risk filming in the actual haunted house, they used another house in New Jersey that looked just like it!

Poltergeists Galore

Poltergeists must be the most common and best documented form of supernatural activity. There are thousands of reports from all around the world, starting in earliest times and continuing right up to the present day.

Almost all poltergeist stories have one factor

in common. They all seem to involve children or young people – very often unhappy adolescent girls. There are two schools of thought about the source of poltergeist activity. Some psychic investigators believe it is caused by psychokinesis – the power of the human mind to move physical objects. The theory is that the mental stresses of adolescence activate some dormant power. The strange noises, slamming doors and flying objects are simply the physical manifestations of the torment in an unhappy teenager's mind.

The more traditional idea is that a poltergeist is an unhappy earth-bound spirit, expressing its frustration with outbreaks of strange noises and pointless destruction.

Demonic possession, an altogether nastier affair, involves an evil spirit struggling to possess a human soul – often, though not always, that of an innocent child. It's up to you which explanation you choose. But if there's an unhappy teenager in your house, convinced that parents and teachers are her deadly enemies and even her best friends hate her – look out for mysterious flying objects!

Roadside Phantoms

Phantom hitch-hikers are a kind of urban myth – those strange stories which all really happened to someone somebody else knows – and stories about these roadside spirits are reported all over the world.

A Ghost in India

In Peshawar in India, a motor-cycle policeman saw a girl walking along a lonely road late at night. Worried about her safety, he gave her a lift home. But before they reached the place where she said she lived, the girl had vanished from the back of his motor bike.

Next day the puzzled policeman checked the files at his police station – and found a photograph of the girl. She had been killed some time ago in a car accident – at the very spot where he'd stopped to pick her up.

The Persistent Ghost

One night in 1982, Haiz Rassen, an Arab merchant living in Puerto Rico, was driving home. He saw a balding man in grey shirt and brown trousers, hitch-hiking by the roadside. Haiz didn't usually like to pick up hitch-hikers – but at the next red light his car engine stalled. As the car stopped he saw the man open the passenger door and get in.

The man, who said his name was Roberto, begged Haiz to help him by driving him to his home. He said he hadn't seen his wife Esperanza and his little boy for two months. At first Haiz refused, but Roberto pleaded with him. Finally Haiz agreed to take him – not all the way home but as far as a nearby restaurant. The car started again and he drove away.

On the way Roberto told Haiz to drive carefully, warned him not to drink, and asked him to pray for him. When they reached the restaurant Haiz turned to his passenger to say they'd arrived. There was no one there. Haiz was so shocked that he collapsed, and someone called the police. Recovering, he managed to tell them his story. The police took him to the address Roberto had originally given. The door was answered by a woman called Esperanza, carrying a little boy. She told the police that she was a widow. Her husband Roberto had been killed in a car accident two months ago. He'd been wearing brown trousers and a grey shirt when he died – and he was partly bald...

The Phantom Accident

One night in 1974 a motorist was driving along on Bluebell Hill, near Chatham. A young girl suddenly appeared in his headlights. He braked as hard as he could, but couldn't avoid hitting her. Horrified, he jumped out of the car and saw her bleeding body lying unconscious beside the road. Not daring to move her, he wrapped her in a blanket and drove off to fetch help. When he returned with the police the blanket was there but the girl was gone. There were no bloodstains and a police tracker dog found no trace of the girl. No injured girl arrived at any hospital that night.

Nine years before, on that very spot, a young bride had been killed on the eve of her wedding. Perhaps the bride-to-be was trying to finish her journey...

A Ghostly Warning

Sometimes, as we've seen, apparitions are connected to an earlier accident. Sometimes they come to deliver a warning. Two such incidents occurred in France.

In 1981, a car stopped to pick up a young woman on a lonely road. Since the car was already full, the girl had to squeeze in the back seat *between* two women passengers. As the car drove along the twisting road she suddenly shouted, "Look out, you're risking death!" and disappeared.

In 1976 two young men in a new sports car stopped to pick up a young woman. It was a two-door car, so the passenger had to get out and push his seat back to allow her to get into the cramped back seat. The driver sped away, and after a while the passenger warned him against driving so fast.

"There have been lots of accidents round here, people have been killed." Not wanting to worry her, the driver slowed down on the next bend. "Other people may be killed here," he said. "But we got by all right." When there was no reply he glanced over his shoulder. The back seat was empty – with no way the hitchhiker could have got out.

Resurrection Mary

The oldest-established roadside phantom operates in Chicago. She's been travelling the highway since the 30s. Known as Resurrection Mary, she's said to be the ghost of a young woman who had a row with her boyfriend, stormed out of his apartment, tried to hitch a lift, and got killed by a speeding car. She was buried in Chicago's Resurrection Cemetery. Now she haunts the highway, still trying to hitch a lift. Perhaps she wants to get back to her boyfriend and win that argument.

The Ghost of Lakey's Creek

A sinister headless horseman, a phantom of the road from earlier times, rode the trail in pioneer days in Illinois. A settler called Lakey had a lonely cabin near a creek. One day he was found murdered, his head severed by his own axe. The axe was still embedded in the tree-trunk by his body. The murder was never solved, but one night some time later, two riders passing the deserted cabin were joined by a headless horseman on a giant black steed. Too terrified to speak, the travellers rode on. The headless figure followed them to the ford where they crossed the creek, then it turned off, and disappeared, apparently into the water . . .

When they told the locals their story, the travellers learned that several others had seen the apparition. It always joined riders to the creek, followed them to the ford and disappeared.

But it seems the headless horseman only ceased to ride when a bridge was built over the creek, and horses were replaced by cars. Perhaps he just couldn't keep up.

CHAPTER 2
SOME FEARSOME FIRES

We turn now from the horrors of the supernatural world to something very real – if not exactly solid – and few things are more frightening than fire. Perhaps it's because, of all natural perils, fire seems the most alive – as if it had an evil intelligence of its own . . . Fires come in all kinds, from national catastrophes to more individual tragedies. Here are a few of the most terrifying.

Rome Burns – AD 64

One of the earliest, and still one of the most famous, fires on record is the burning of Rome in AD 64. This is the one the Emperor Nero is supposed to have fiddled to – although historically speaking, he's much more likely to have played the lyre. Apparently he sang at the same time. (Nero fancied himself greatly as singer, musician and poet – and since it was life-threatening to criticize the emperor, no one ever disillusioned him.)

Two things make this fire particularly terrible. The first is the fact that it was started deliberately – almost certainly at the orders of Nero himself. The second is its horrifying aftermath. Rome had more than its share of mad emperors, but Nero was undoubtedly one of the maddest. Quite why he started the fire isn't clear. One theory is that he needed more room to expand his enormous palace, which already occupied two of Rome's seven hills. Another idea is that it was an early slum-clearance scheme. Or perhaps it was just because he was raving mad and liked fires – pyromania on an imperial scale.

Whatever the reason, the blaze began mysteriously at the Circus Maximus and spread rapidly through the narrow, crowded streets, helped by a strong wind.

Roman historian Tacitus has left us a contemporary account: "Terrified, shrieking women and the helpless, old and young, all added to the confusion. Wherever people looked, forwards or back, they found themselves cut off by fire. When they tried to escape to districts they thought safe, the fire followed them."

Tacitus makes it clear that the fire was started deliberately: "People who tried to fight the fire were stopped by gangs of threatening thugs. Men were seen throwing burning torches into buildings. They said they were acting under orders."

The fire gained such a strong foothold that it threatened to burn down the whole of Rome. Eventually even Nero realized that he had

gone too far, and allowed Rome's official fire brigades to go into action. They couldn't do much about the fire itself, but by destroying buildings in its path they stopped it from spreading even further. By the time the blaze died down it had totally destroyed three of Rome's fourteen districts and seriously damaged three more. Temples and other old buildings that had stood since Rome was founded over eight hundred years before were completely consumed. It's not known how many were killed and injured – the total must have run into hundreds, perhaps thousands.

Rumours of the emperor's involvement spread rapidly and soon the angry Roman mob was after Nero's blood. There was a very good chance that they'd get it too. Nero knew well that being Emperor of Rome was far from a safe position. Many an earlier Emperor had come to a sudden and sticky end, when the people turned against him.

What Nero needed was a scapegoat, and

fortunately for him there was a good one close at hand. He decided to blame the fire on the members of one of Rome's many religious cults. This particular one was called Christianity.

Proclaiming loudly that the Christians were responsible for the fire and ignoring the absence of any proof, Nero ordered mass arrests. The arrests were followed by mass crucifixions. Not satisfied with crucifixion, Nero decided that the Christians' punishment ought to fit their alleged crime. Soon more smoke blackened the skies of Rome as Christian captives were coated in tar, tied to poles set up in Nero's gardens, and set ablaze. To entertain the mob other victims were wrapped in animal skins and thrust into the arena to be torn to pieces by wild beasts.

Having appeased the angry citizens by the traditional Roman recipe of "Bread and Circuses" Nero set about rebuilding his palace on an even grander scale, for now that he had plenty of room, he could spread out a bit. With a typically modest touch, he put a statue of himself, 120 feet high, in the entrance hall. The enormous gardens contained a number of lakes and several complete forests, as well as a mile-long arcade lined with pillars.

Nero also rebuilt much of Rome, using fireproof materials like stone, and designing the new buildings and city streets so that the fire brigades would have easy access. After all, he didn't want to risk a fire burning down his nice new palace . . .

The Great Fire of London – 1666

Another capital city badly damaged in a famous historical fire was London. The Great Fire started in Pudding Lane on 2 September 1666, and ended at Pie Corner – five days later. Pudding Lane was where John Farynor, who happened to be the royal baker, had his shop. Tired after a long hard day, he neglected to make sure his oven was properly damped down before going to bed.

In the middle of the night, woken by cries of "Fire!", he went outside and saw sparks streaming from his chimney. Unfortunately some of them landed on a pile of hay stacked up against the wall of the nearby pub, called the Star. The hay was blazing merrily – and soon afterwards so was the pub.

It was even more unfortunate that London had just been undergoing a long dry spell. Timbers of building were preserved in pitch in those days, and the walls made of lathe and plaster – all highly inflammable. A crowd

The Great Fire of London

gathered to watch the blaze, but there was no particular panic, not at first. Fires were by no means uncommon in seventeenth-century London and, just as in ancient Rome, fire brigades existed to deal with the problem.

King Charles II, newly restored to his throne after Oliver Cromwell's revolution, had issued orders that stricter fire regulations were to be enforced. Unfortunately, nobody had taken very much notice.

Aided by a strong wind, the Pudding Lane fire spread towards the river Thames – which was lined with warehouses, filled with all kinds of highly inflammable goods. Belatedly mindful of the king's orders, city officials roused the Lord Mayor of London. They told him that the fire was threatening the main London Bridge Road. Grumbling, the Lord Mayor turned out and went to inspect the blaze. He wasn't much impressed. "A woman might piss it out," he said scathingly and went back to bed. He'd underestimated the situation badly. The fire spread and spread.

There's an excellent eyewitness account of this particular fire. It comes from Samuel Pepys, the famous diarist, then Secretary to the Admiralty. Pepys first heard of the fire from his excited servants and went to the window to take a look at it. He saw the still-distant blaze, decided, like the Lord Mayor, that there was nothing much to worry about, and went back to bed. Next morning at breakfast his wife told him that the fire was still blazing. Three hundred houses had been destroyed and all of Fish Street by the Thames had been burned down. Pepys made his way down to the Thames, hired a boat, and went to see for himself.

He discovered what he called a "lamentable fire", with people only concerned to save their goods and get them into boats and barges on the river. No one seemed to be doing anything about trying to tackle the fire itself. He wrote: "Having stayed and in an hour's time seen the fire rage every way, and nobody, to my sight, endeavouring to quench it, but to remove their goods and leave everything to the fire, and the wind mighty high and driving into the city, and everything, after so long a drought, proving combustible, even the very stones of churches . . ."

Realizing at last the full seriousness of the situation, Pepys hurried to the Palace of Whitehall. Thanks to his position as a top civil servant, he was able to gain access to the king. The king saw at once that the only solution was the one adopted by the Romans over a thousand years before. If the fire couldn't be put out, it must be contained. The houses in its path must be pulled down. Pepys and other messengers hurried about the city, passing on the king's orders. Pepys encountered the Lord Mayor, who had now revised his estimate of the situation:

"To the King's message he cried like a fainting woman, 'Lord! What can I do? I am spent, the people will not obey me. I have been pulling down houses but the fire overtakes us faster than we can do it.'"

Pepys saw how crowded together the houses were. The whole area was "full of matter for burning, as pitch and tar in Thames Street, and warehouses of oil and wines and brandy."

Fanned by strong winds, the fire raged on for five days. Samuel Pepys paints a vivid picture of the blaze:

"All over the Thames, with one's faces in the wind you were almost burned with a shower of firedrops. The fire, as it grew darker, appeared more and more, in corners, and upon steeples and between churches and in houses as far as we could see up the hill of the city in a most horrid malicious bloody flame . . .

"We saw the fire as only one arch of fire, from this to the other side of the bridge, and in a bow up the hill for an arch of above a mile long. It made me weep to see it. The churches, houses and all on fire and flaming at once, and a horrid noise the flame made and the crackling of houses . . ."

He writes of walking in Moorfields, "Our feet ready to burn walking through the town among hot coals, full of people and poor wretches carrying their goods . . ."

Led by the king himself, and by his brother the Duke of York, the battle against the fire raged on. By now things were so bad that houses in the path of the flames were being blown up rather than just pulled down. At last the wind died down, and so did the fire. It was time to take stock of the damage: 13 000 houses had burned down, and 87 churches, St Paul's Cathedral amongst them; the Royal Exchange, the Guildhall and other public buildings had been destroyed; 400 city streets had been completely wiped out. Astonishingly, only 8 people had been killed. Severe as it was, the fire had started slowly. London was much smaller then and Londoners had had time to get away to the safety of the country.

There was one unexpected benefit, but it was a big one. For years bubonic plague had been ravaging Europe. After the Great Fire, the Great Plague virtually vanished from

England – though it continued in Europe for another hundred years. The fierce heat of the flames had destroyed the bacteria that caused the plague, along with the rats and their fleas that carried the disease.

Fire seems to be one of the hazards of civilization. As cities grew bigger, more crowded and more industrialized, the hazards of fire grew ever greater. More and more regulations were introduced, and fire-fighting methods improved – but somehow the fire, like some malignant demon, stayed one step ahead. As events in Chicago showed, it didn't do to be over-confident.

The Great Chicago Fire – 1871

You might say Chicago was used to fires. After all, the Chicago of 1871 was a city made largely of wood, right down to the planked wooden pavements. The city expected fires from time to time, and it was ready to deal with them.

A big, bustling city of 30 000 inhabitants, Chicago was bang up-to-date. It prided itself on having one of the most modern fire departments in the world. There were no less than seventeen horse-drawn fire carriages and twenty-three hose-carts.

There were telegraph alarm boxes dotted about the city, and a man on top of the court-house roof, keeping an eye out for smoke. What more could anyone want? Sadly, it wasn't enough.

Just as in Rome, and in London, Chicago's Great Fire was preceded by a long, hot, dry spell. There had been quite a few fires already but the fire department had coped. But they weren't prepared for Mrs O'Leary's cow.

Mrs O'Leary kept her cow in a barn on De Koven street, on the west side of the city. Someone left an oil lamp alight in the barn and, on the night of 8 December 1871, the cow kicked over the lamp. The straw caught fire and very soon several nearby houses were ablaze.

At this point Murphy's law came into operation – what can go wrong will! Someone tried to use the alarm signal box. It wasn't working. What about the man on the courthouse roof? Well, he spotted the smoke right enough, but he got so excited that he sent the fire brigade in the wrong direction. By the time they managed to find the fire it had spread to cover an entire city block. The firemen did their best, but the fire was well established, the wooden city was tinder-dry and there was a strong wind blowing. Before very long not one but twenty city blocks were ablaze.

By the following morning the fire had spread across the Chicago river into the narrow crowded streets of the slum areas on the other side. The area was filled with bars and brothels, and angry, drunken customers started fights with the weary firemen.

The fire spread to the main business district. It even burned down Chicago's pride and joy – the new marble courthouse, which was supposed to be fireproof. Soon it reached the lake, setting several ships on fire.

Then came Chicago's last, and worst piece of bad luck. Wind carried burning debris across the river and it landed on the roof of the waterworks. The waterworks caught fire and burned to the ground – which meant no more

water supplies to the firefighters.

The Chicago Fire Department was beaten. Its resources were exhausted. All it could do was stand back and watch the city burn.

The fire burned on all day and into the night. At last the wind dropped and it started to rain. The fire died down finally and the shocked citizens of Chicago took stock of the damage. The entire centre of Chicago had been destroyed – an area covering about 4 square miles. Considering the crowded conditions and the sheer scale of the fire, the loss of life was comparatively low – somewhere between 250 and 300 deaths.

The O'Learys, whose cow, you remember, had caused all the trouble, were amongst the survivors. Although their barn burned down, their house was untouched by the blaze. It wasn't so much the

fire as the aftermath that endangered the O'Learys' lives. When the story got out, an angry crowd surrounded their house determined to lynch them. The police wouldn't allow it, though the firemen were probably all for it.

For some reason the citizens' anger was aimed mainly at Mr O'Leary, husband of the owner of the cow. Eventually it affected him so much, he left Chicago in disguise. No one knows what happened to the cow . . .

Not every fire devastates an entire city. Smaller, more localized blazes – and there are hundreds, thousands, every year – can still be major tragedies to those involved. One of the worst recorded fires happened in New York.

The Triangle Factory Fire – 1911

The Triangle Shirtwaist Factory was a typical sweatshop of the time. It manufactured shirtwaists – ladies' blouses – and it was situated on the top three floors of the ten-storey Asch Building in New York. Young women and girls, most of them between 14 and 20 worked at long lines of sewing machines. They came mostly from poor immigrant families. They spoke little English and worked long hours for very low pay.

If working conditions were bad, safety conditions were even worse. There were four lifts, but only one of them worked properly. There were two stairways to the street, one leading to Greene Street, the other to Washington Place. The doors to the street at the bottom of both staircases were locked. There was a semi-derelict fire-escape, only 18 inches wide. There were a few fire-buckets of water along the walls. There *was* a fire-hose but it had rotted away from neglect. There was a No Smoking sign, but it was frequently ignored. New York City Fire Inspectors were well aware of the fire-risks in the many factories of this kind. They had made many protests. Factory owners couldn't be bothered to spend time and money on safety precautions. Regulations were hard to enforce. The manufacturers were rich and influential, and the New York City authorities weren't really interested in upsetting them.

At the end of the day on a Saturday, several workers were putting on their coats ready to go home. Somehow a small fire started in a rag bin on the eighth floor. Nobody quite knows how, though it seems likely someone had thrown in the still-smouldering butt of an illicit cigarette.

The blaze took hold and someone yelled "fire!". Two men ran up with fire-buckets, but the fire was already too well established. Some others tried to unroll the fire hose. The valve was jammed shut and the hose fell to pieces in their hands.

Bales of cloth and rows of garments lined the corridors and crowded the cramped factory premises. The whole place was filled with highly inflammable material. The fire leaped from the rag bin and up to the racks of clothes hanging from the ceiling, and moved on to the cutting tables. The smoke-filled corridor leading to the one working lift became jammed with screaming, terrified young women. The lift could only take twelve at a time. After a few trips burned-out cables put it out of action. Panic-stricken girls threw themselves down the lift-shaft to their deaths.

The fire spread to the ninth floor, and began threatening the tenth, which was occupied by suites of offices. One of the owners was being visited by his children, accompanied by their governess. They all managed to escape by using a fire-ladder as a bridge to the roof of the neighbouring building.

Meanwhile most of the factory girls were trapped on the two blazing floors below. Some ran for the stairs leading to the Greene Street exit, and desperately struggling bodies piled up by the locked door at the bottom. Somehow they wrenched the doors open and stumbled out to safety. Those who tried the Washington Square exit weren't so lucky. The doors stayed firmly shut. The fire roared down the crowded stairwell, burning them to death. Others tried the fire escape. Warped by the heat the iron ladder gave way, hurling them to the ground, eight floors below.

By the time the firemen arrived, frantic women were jumping in clusters from the windows. A firemen said it seemed to be raining bodies. There were so many broken bodies on the pavements that it was difficult for the firemen to unwind their hoses. Safety ladders were raised, but they were useless. They reached only to the seventh floor and the terrified girls couldn't get to them. Many fell to the ground in the attempt.

Safety nets were spread, but the weight of the girls' hurtling bodies smashed through them. A reporter wrote that the water from the firemen's hoses ran in the gutter, red with blood.

In under twenty minutes, it was all over. Firemen chopped down the doors and put out the flames. They found the ninth floor filled with blackened corpses. There were still more at the foot of the lift shaft. Over 50 broken bodies lay on the pavement; altogether 145 young girls lost their lives.

Even hard-boiled New York exploded in sorrow and anger. There was a mass funeral for the victims, attended by 10 000 mourners. The owners of the factory were put on trial for manslaughter – and acquitted. The locked doors, said the grand jury, "might have been locked by an employee".

There was a further storm of indignation led by New York's popular newspapers. A union was formed and new Fire Prevention Laws were passed. Slowly things started to improve. It was still a case of too little and too late, however – and it was too late by far for the girls at the Triangle Shirtwaist Factory.

Fire is an ever-present image in modern warfare. The Second World War was often called "The World in Flames". Organizing Europe's resistance to Nazi occupation, Winston Churchill's command was "Set Europe ablaze!" From the destruction of Warsaw at the war's very beginning, to the flames that almost destroyed Berlin at its end, fire, used as a weapon, ravaged many a city during the Second World War. By far the worst of these fires happened at the very end of the war. It was caused, not by the Nazis, but by our side, the Allies.

Dresden — 1945

Oddly enough, it all started with the Russians. By 1945 the war was nearly over. Russian troops were advancing towards Berlin. But the German Army wasn't beaten yet. It was still putting up unexpectedly strong resistance. At the Allied conference in Yalta, the Russians asked their British and American allies for help. In particular they asked for air attacks in the area ahead of their advance, to destroy German communications. The Allied Chiefs of Staff agreed to do whatever they could to help the attacking Soviet Army. They decided on air strikes against the German Army's lines of communications in the Berlin, Leipzig and Dresden regions.

Put like this, it all sounds logical enough. What actually happened to Dresden is a very different matter. By a terrible irony, Dresden in 1945 was regarded as one of the safest cities in Germany. It was an old town, of no particular strategic importance, filled with historic buildings including art galleries, churches and a magnificent cathedral. Dresden was packed with refugees, fleeing from the advancing Russians. In addition, 26 000 Allied prisoners of war were being held there. The town was so overcrowded that prison camps had been set up in the parks.

Back in 1940, with German victories everywhere, the British looked much more like losing than winning the war. The Luftwaffe, the German air force, bombed the cathedral city of Coventry. The raid destroyed 27 factories,

killed over 500 people, and started a colossal fire that wiped out the city centre. Because of this, 400 of those killed were too badly burned to be identified and had to be buried all together in one mass grave. The triumphant Nazis coined a new word, to "Coventryize" an enemy town – to wipe it out. "Bomber" Harris, later head of Britain's Bomber Command, said grimly that the Germans had taught us a useful bombing technique – starting so many fires at once that no fire service could possibly cope. It was a lesson he never forgot.

Three years later, "Bomber" Harris made use of that lesson. The Allies bombed Hamburg, using vast numbers of incendiary bombs. A British pilot who flew on the raid said there were so many fires that they merged into "a turbulent dome of red fire, lighted and ignited like the glowing heart of a vast brazier". This time, it was the turn of the Hamburg Fire Department to coin a terrible new word – "Firestorm". A Hamburg factory worker called it "a massive sea of fire". At the centre of the fire, hurricane-force winds sprang up, driving the fire forward with irresistible force. Unable to escape this inferno, 42 000 people were killed and 8 square miles of the city centre were totally destroyed.

There seems little doubt that the bombing of

Dresden was deliberately designed to produce the same firestorm effect.

On the night of 13 February 1943, over 200 British bombers attacked Dresden, followed soon afterwards by over 500 more. 13 February was Shrove Tuesday, a date traditionally celebrated as a festival in Germany. Lots of parties were still going on when the first bombers arrived. The Luftwaffe had very few night-fighters available. By the time the bombers were spotted and air-raid warnings sounded it was far too late.

The justification for the raid, and target for the Allied bombs, was the railway marshalling yards. This first raid created a firestorm which raged through 11 square miles of the city. Thirty-six hours after the raid, with the city still in flames, and the fire-services desperately trying to cope, there was a second raid by 200 American bombers. Soon all of Dresden was in flames – fires burned for seven days and nights. The flames of the burning city could be seen for miles around. It was a terrible shock for Germans everywhere. Never before had Allied bombers struck so deep in the heart of Germany itself. In nearby prison and labour camps, captives saw it and rejoiced, knowing that the end of Nazi Germany must be near.

Strangely enough, there's a celebrity eye-witness to the bombing of Dresden. The American writer Kurt Vonnegut, later to be famous as the author of *Slaughterhouse Five*, was a prisoner in a nearby camp. He was one of the working-parties brought into the city to clear up when the fires started to die down.

"Every day we walked into the city and dug into basements and shelters to get corpses out," he later recalled. He describes finding whole rooms filled with unmarked dead bodies. "Just people sitting there in their chairs, all dead."

Similar strange deaths had been observed after the bombing of Hamburg. It seems that they were a freak effect of the firestorm — caused, perhaps by intense heat, and the sudden removal of oxygen from the atmosphere. Small wonder that Kurt Vonnegut's best-selling novel *Slaughterhouse Five*, written many years later, was a kind of black comedy, a savage and gruesome satire on the madness of war.

Vonnegut was luckier than he realized at the time. Adolf Hitler was so enraged by the destruction of Dresden that he ordered the execution of all the Allied prisoners in its camps. Fortunately, his Nazi advisers managed to talk him out of it. They knew in their hearts that the war was as good as lost by now. With Allied armies fast approaching Berlin, this was no time to start shooting allied prisoners.

Nobody knows quite how many people died in Dresden. The Dresden police gave a first estimate of 18 000, with more to follow. Later estimates put the figure as high as 130 000. The Dresden authorities identified nearly 40 000 bodies, most of them burned to death.

Dresden destroyed

Over 20 000 other bodies, so badly burned as to be unidentifiable, were found in the ruins.

A final total in the region of at least 70 000 seems most likely. The monument on the mass grave in Dresden Cemetery bears the simple inscription: "How many died? Who knows the number?"

In the years following the war, the once-accepted tactic of bombing the enemy's cities became steadily more controversial. In the emotive atmosphere of wartime, things seemed very different. People who'd seen London in flames during the "Blitz", as the Nazi bombing campaign was called, weren't going to be too upset later on, when Germany got a dose of the same medicine.

But as time went on, people got more and more worried about the morality of it all. When the war was over, it was admitted by both sides that bombing, especially night-bombing, wasn't nearly as accurate as had been claimed. Military objectives were always the target of course – munitions factories, arms depots, railways and so on. But when the target was missed, as it often was, it was the civilians nearby who suffered.

The controversy still goes on. Not long ago, a proposal to put up a statue to Air-Marshal "Bomber" Harris aroused a storm of protest –

not just in Germany but in England as well.

Dresden will remain on the conscience of the Allies for years to come. Apart from the atomic bombing of Hiroshima and Nagasaki, Dresden is still the most controversial of all Allied bombing raids – and the hardest to justify to posterity.

After all, it can be argued that the dropping of the atomic bomb forced Japan to surrender and shortened the war. What did the bombing of Dresden achieve? The purpose of the raid, remember, was to destroy the railway marshalling yards. Two days after the attack, trains were once again running through Dresden.

Fire Down Under

In peacetime as in war, the menace of fire is still with us. It's scarcely surprising that terrible firestorms rage when men drop explosives to start them on purpose. But fire can devastate places that take every possible precaution to prevent them.

Australia is one of the worst sufferers of all. The intense heat of its climate makes fire a potential hazard at the best of times. The widespread eucalyptus tree doesn't help much either: its leaves are rich in oil. and in bush fires the trees explode into raging firebombs, hurling flaming particles through the air and spreading the blaze.

When conditions are even worse than usual, as they occasionally are, the fire-risk is enormous. There can be few more terrifying events than an Australian bush fire.

Fire in the Wind

6 February 1851 was an exceptionally hot day, even for Southern Australia. Temperatures of 112°F were recorded in several areas around Melbourne. In the nearby town of Kilmore, the hot wind blew clouds of suffocating dust through the town. Fires started in the surrounding dry grass and the wind sent balls of burning grass drifting over the town, starting several other fires. Not far away, in Portland, the surrounding grass-fires sent fiery particles drifting over the town, and the townsfolk could smell the burning sheep and cattle on the outlying farms.

In Melbourne, the temperature rose to 117°F. Black smoke swirled over the roof-tops and the streets were filled with ash. In the wooded mountain ranges of Cape Otway, a fierce fire roared through the gum trees.

The fire, or rather a whole series of fires, spread rapidly. A pall of smoke descended on the entire area, turning day into night. The Aborigines said there was a blight on the sun. Fire swept through the settlements around the Dandenong Hills, leaving only one house standing. Everywhere houses, barns and stables were destroyed, with over a hundred families left homeless. Mobs of panic-stricken wild horses thundered over the burning plains desperate to escape the fire. In the evening the wind changed and rain began to fall. It took a long time to repair the damage and get things back to normal. Ever afterwards, the people of Melbourne called 6 February 1851, "Black Thursday".

"Black Thursday" wasn't the first bush fire Australian settlers had to cope with and of course it wasn't the last. The danger of bush fires is a part of Australian life. As the years went by the Australian authorities developed more and more sophisticated ways of dealing with them. Today each state has its own fire department, with early warning systems, helicopters, state-of-the-art firefighting equipment.

You might think that with all this modern technology, the bush fire, terrifying in 1851, was no longer much of a menace. You'd be wrong.

Summer of '83

Just as in 1851, the summer of 1983 was exceptionally hot, – even by Australian standards. This didn't matter so much in the really remote areas known as the Outback. Arid and harsh at the best of times, there just wasn't much to burn. It was largely uninhabited as well – except of  course by the Australian native peoples, the Aborigines, who have their own mysterious methods of survival, however hot the weather.

It was the bush that was in trouble, the region between the coastal cities and the central Outback. This is an area of scrubby grassland, little towns and remote farms. In 1983, after months without rain it was as dry as a tinder-box.

The state authorities were well aware of the

danger. Throwing away a match or a cigarette end could get you a heavy fine, or even a prison sentence. And there weren't just such obvious hazards to worry about. It was almost as dangerous to throw away an old bottle. A bit of broken glass could magnify the blazing rays of the sun and set a tuft of dry grass smouldering. It was all it would take . . .

The first bush fires broke out in a remote hill area, where the temperature had just touched 110° Fahrenheit in the shade. And as the old Australian joke goes, there wasn't any shade. Three other outbreaks followed in Victoria, then three more in Adelaide. In spite of all the preparations and precautions, there wasn't much anyone could do. With the wind behind them bush fires can travel at 70 miles an hour. They can cross roads and rivers. Almost nothing can stop them.

One little town found itself directly in the path of the fire. The owner of an outlying property had only a few minutes to evacuate before his house went up in flames. Some inhabitants tried to escape by car. Many of them were overtaken by the flames and burned alive in their cars. Others stayed put, hiding in their cellars and hoping the fires would pass over them. One family jumped into their huge water tank to escape – only to find that the heat of the fires was starting to boil the water. Luckily the fire moved past before they were cooked. When the local school was surrounded by flames the children survived by lying down under water-soaked blankets, while parents and teachers dampened the school roof with hoses.

Alarms had gone out by now, and soon the state fire services came to the rescue with helicopters. Twenty-nine people died, and most of the little town was destroyed.

Soon there were bush fires blazing all over Southern Australia – some of them stretching over hundreds of miles. More fleeing motorists were burned alive in their cars as the fast-moving flames caught up with them. In Melbourne, one of Southern Australia's major cities, people could see the approaching smoke only 20 miles away. Plans were made to dig massive trenches all around the town to act as firebreaks.

An entire forest caught fire, defying the efforts of over 7000 firefighters. A little seaside resort town was completely destroyed by fire. The inhabitants took refuge on the beach – and watched in amazement as kangaroos and other animals, driven before the flames, hurled themselves over the cliffs and into the sea.

Well-organized and well-prepared, the Fire Service gradually got the upper hand. Slowly the flames came under control. When it was all over there were over seventy dead, and over 8000 homes destroyed. The number of sheep and cattle lost was 200 000, and countless kangaroos, koalas, and other forms of Australian wildlife were killed by the fire. The Prime Minister, Malcolm Fraser, declared a state of emergency. Special aid was promised for destroyed towns and ruined farmers and home owners.

There was national concern about the causes of the fire. There was wild talk of arson, though by whom and for what reason remained obscure. One theory was that sparks from electric cables might have caused the blaze. It might equally have been that dropped cigarette end or the sun through that piece of glass.

It had been the worst bush fire in Australian history to date. But it wasn't the first, nor would it be the last. Not as long as that Australian sun goes on beating down on the parched dry bush. It's not all fun, living in the land of sunshine.

Fire Today

The menace of fire has been with us throughout history. And, of course, it's still with us today. Look in any newspaper and you'll see accounts of domestic fires caused by carelessly used oil heaters and faulty electric appliances – often with horrific loss of life.

And, of course, some fires are started on purpose. Not so long ago a man was refused admission to a seedy backstreet cinema. He came back with a can of petrol and a box of matches. In the horrific blaze, dozens of lives were lost.

The biggest cause of fire is probably sheer carelessness. A dropped cigarette end can still cause a terrible catastrophe – even if you're not living in the sun-baked Australian bush . . .

The King's Cross Disaster

The horrific events at King's Cross illustrate the insidious nature of fire. The way it can lurk, biding its time, while people grow careless and precautions are relaxed – and then strike with sudden devastating force.

King's Cross is one of London's busiest and most important stations. There are two main line terminals side by side, St Pancras, and King's Cross itself. King's Cross is also an important junction on the Underground. Five different underground lines come together here – Piccadilly, Northern, Metropolitan, Victoria, and Circle. Every day thousands of passengers pass through King's Cross station, changing from one Underground line to another,

or getting out to catch a train at one of the two main-line stations. The station is busiest, of course, during morning and evening rush hours.

Beneath the old-fashioned wooden escalator that led from the Piccadilly line to the main line there was an area of unused space. Although the escalator itself was regularly serviced and maintained, no one seems to have bothered to clean out the area below. Over long years, the once-empty space had gradually become choked with all kinds of debris. The rubbish was soaked with oil and grease from the escalator.

For a long time the British had been very tolerant about smoking. People were allowed to smoke in cinemas and upstairs on buses. They were also allowed to smoke in Underground stations and they could smoke on the trains too, as long as it wasn't a non-smoking compartment.

Sometime on 18 November 1987, probably during the afternoon, one of two things must have happened:

Someone riding the Piccadilly escalator lit a cigarette, dropped the still-burning match down through the gap besides the moving treads and went on their way.

Or someone took the last drag from a cigarette and dropped the glowing cigarette end down the same gap. Whichever was the case, what may have seemed a simple piece of thoughtlessness turned out to be a criminally careless act. It had the same effect as lighting the fuse on a bomb.

The match, or cigarette end, set light to the oil-soaked rubbish. It smouldered quietly, completely unnoticed, for several hours. Then it burst into flames. At 7.50 p.m., just as the rush hour was coming to an end, the Piccadilly-line escalator was crowded with people riding up to the main ticket hall. Suddenly, smoke began drifting from beneath the escalator. With terrifying speed, a huge fireball erupted from below the stairs, sped up the escalator and exploded by the turnstiles at the top. Very soon the whole of the crowded ticket hall was ablaze.

People began screaming in panic and attempting to flee. Down below, Underground staff directed passengers onto the escalator for the Victoria line – but that too emptied into the blazing turnstile area. "We followed instructions and got on the other escalator," said one survivor. "About half-way up a sheet of flame shot across the top. Soon the ceiling was on fire and debris started falling down."

According to the survivors, most London

Underground staff were as confused as the passengers themselves. Passengers said later that nobody was seen using a fire extinguisher, and no one seemed to be directing the terrified passengers to safety.

The alarm had been given by now, and very soon the London Fire Brigade was on the scene. It took a number of fire engines and 150 firefighters to put out the flames, rescue the passengers from the blaze, and take out the dying and the dead.

The King's Cross blaze is the worst fire in London Underground history. A total of 31 people died and 80 were injured; of these, 20 had to spend some time in hospital. Afterwards there was an enquiry into how and why the fire had happened. London Underground were accused of negligence, and neglect of vital safety precautions. Heads rolled in the higher regions of London Transport. Soon afterwards it was announced that all-metal escalators were to be installed at King's Cross and that millions of pounds would be

spent on new safety equipment. The horse had gone, but at least the stable door was shut.

The terrible tragedy was a major influence in changing attitudes to public smoking. Today it is forbidden to smoke not only on Underground trains themselves, but anywhere in stations. London Transport have finally realized that smoking can harm your health – in more ways than one.

CHAPTER 3
NATURAL HORRORS

We've talked about the supernatural world and about fire, one of the great hazards of nature. But there are lots of other dangers we have cause to worry about. We're not alone on the planet, we share it with all kinds of creatures, great and small. Some are friendly, like cats and dogs, some are useful, like horses and carrier pigeons. Some are cute and cuddly, like rabbits and koalas Quite a few of these animals we eat – so it's only fair that one or two of them occasionally eat us. Because while lots of our fellow creatures are nice, some can be downright nasty. That cat purring by the fire has larger relatives who can rip you to shreds. The friendly dog has a pack of wolfish ancestors who might tear you to pieces. If you've seen Alfred Hitchcock's *The Birds* you'll keep a careful eye on the budgie and Steven Spielberg's *Jaws* will even make you wary about the goldfish. And what's that many-legged creature scuttling under the sofa? Some of the wonders of wildlife are enough to give you the horrors . . .

Spider!

The spider must be one of the most feared and hated creatures on the planet. It isn't really fair, because very few spiders are actually dangerous – not even the big furry ones the size of dinner plates. But it's no use talking to your dedicated arachnophobe (that's Greek for spider hater). The memory of a tarantula crawling across James Bond's bare chest still haunts those who saw *Dr No*, the first Bond film. The innocent domestic spider in the bath can still provoke a shuddering retreat from many of us. Yet even a fairly harmless spider can cause some serious problems . . .

The Horrible Huntsman

One of the commoner spiders in Australia is called the huntsman. It's as big as your hand, hairy and ferocious-looking, with beady black eyes and long sharp fangs. However, it's absolutely harmless. It seldom bites, and even if it does causes little harm. The fangs are big enough to pierce the skin, but the venom, fatal to insects, is so weak that it affects humans no more than a mosquito bite. Yet the huntsman spider often causes damage, injury and occasionally death. How?

Unfortunately the huntsman has a habit of hiding in the little nooks and crannies of motor cars. Sometimes it turns up unexpectedly when the car is moving. Face to face with a great big hairy spider on the dashboard or on the seat, some motorists have decidedly dramatic reactions. They swerve wildly all over the road, crash into other cars, or drive straight at the nearest solid object – like a telephone box, or a tree. Drivers have even been known to jump from their cars while they were still moving, rather than share them with a spider! Every year in Australia the spider-in-the-car syndrome causes a number of dangerous and sometimes fatal car accidents.

As if the huntsman didn't cause enough trouble, Australians have some really dangerous spiders to deal with as well.

The Revolting Red-back

The Australian red-back spider – also found in Africa, America, Asia, New Zealand and even in Southern Europe – is fifteen times more poisonous than a rattlesnake. Unfortunately, these spiders are extremely common in some parts of the world. Even more unfortunately, they're common in places where people live. They like to come into houses and hide in clothes and shoes. They attack when disturbed, biting furiously as often as they can.

Get bitten by one of these and you're really in trouble. Their venom can cause terrible pain, hallucinations and respiratory paralysis. About 300 people get bitten by red-backs every year.

The really traditional hiding place for the red-back is under the toilet seat. Encountering one there is something you don't even want to think about.

The Fearsome Funnel-web

Another Australian nasty is the Sydney funnel-web spider, which is also fond of hiding in houses. It gets its name from the purse-shaped web-trap it spins to catch its prey.

With the funnel-web it's the male spider that's most dangerous. With most other spider species its the other way round. As Kipling said:

"The female of the species Is more deadly than the male."

If you should run into a Sydney funnel-web, don't think it's going to scuttle away and hide. Funnel-webs have absolutely no fear of people – they just rear up and strike with savage force. A funnel-web can strike hard enough to drive its fangs through a human finger-nail. Their venom produces numbness of the mouth and tongue, nausea and even coma.

Today effective anti-venom remedies are available for most spider bites. Actual deaths are rare. The last two recorded fatalities took place in 1979 when a young woman died and in 1980 when the victim was a two-year-old child.

The Big Boys

The largest spiders in the world are the so-called bird-eating spiders found in Africa and South America. (No one's ever actually seen them eating birds – they're called that because they look as if they could. In reality, like other spiders they feed mostly on insects.) One of the largest ever recorded was found by an expedition in Venezuela in 1965. With a body length of 9 centimetres and a leg-span of 28 centimetres, this one really was a big as a dinner plate.

Despite their great size and fearsome appearance, bird-eating spiders aren't really dangerous to humans – their venom is comparatively weak. It just isn't true that the bigger and hairier the spider the more dangerous it is – the smaller ones can sometimes be the worst.

Brazil Wanderers

One of the world's nastiest specimens has to be the wandering spider of Brazil. Big and black and highly dangerous, this spider gets its name because it doesn't bother about building webs. It just comes wandering out at night looking for its prey.

Like the funnel-web it has no fear of humans. Meet one and it's more likely to attack than to run away. Also like the funnel-web it's often found hiding in houses,

in clothes and in shoes. Its venom is highly dangerous, and can cause respiratory failure and even heart attacks.

Spider Dance

Europe too has its share of dangerous spiders. One particular species of spider, associated with the town of Taranto in Southern Italy, is called the tarantula. In the Middle Ages the tarantula was said to have caused astonishing outbreaks of public dancing. According to the story, those bitten by this spider immediately broke out into a violent dance, apparently with the intention of flushing the venom from their bodies. The practice went on for hundreds of years, and gave rise to a lively and energetic dance called the tarantella which became popular all over Europe.

Sting!

Just as frightening as the spider, but far less common is the scorpion, a prehistoric-looking creature with its sting curving over its back in a long tail. Scorpions are common in tropical countries, and they're very dangerous. Their natural habitat is the dark and shady areas under rocks, but they're quite happy in houses as well. They come into kitchens looking for food or water. Damp attracts them and they turn up inside taps and in toilet bowls. A scorpion is fully as venomous as a cobra. Its overhanging tail is tremendously strong, and can drive the pointed sting through clothes and even shoes. A scorpion bite produces a burning pain which gives way to a strong tingling sensation. This is followed by fast breathing, sneezing and sweating, respiratory paralysis, and even death. Scorpians abound in

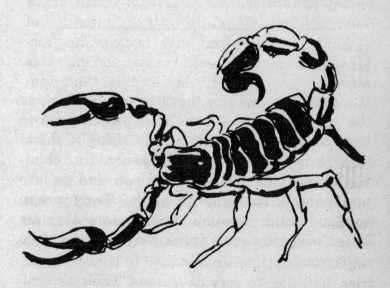

Tunisia, where, according to the local authorities, at least 20 000 people were stung in the forties and fifties, and over 400 of them died. Today, as with snake and spider bites, prompt treatment with anti-venom has lowered the death rate. The Tunisian Government operates a cash-on-the-tail bounty system, paying local people and school-children to catch scorpions and hand them in. (That's earning your pocket money the hard way.) Many thousands are handed in every year and their venom used to produce anti-venom. Despite this the Tunisian scorpion continues to spread and thrive.

Hiss!

If there's one creature that's feared as much as the spider it's the snake. Most people seem to have an instinctive fear and loathing of them. (Maybe it's something in the genes. Our chim-panzee cousins shout and scream and go into total panic at the sight of a snake.) Every year in England hundreds of harmless grass snakes are killed because people think they just might be dangerous.

England's Adder

The adder, or viper, is England's only poisonous snake. Compared to other poisonous snakes, its record is fairly mild. It has only killed 10 people in England since 1890; 6 of these were small children. The most recent death from snakebite in the British Isles was also that of a child, a five-year-old died after being bitten by a viper at Callender in Perthshire.

Australia's Record

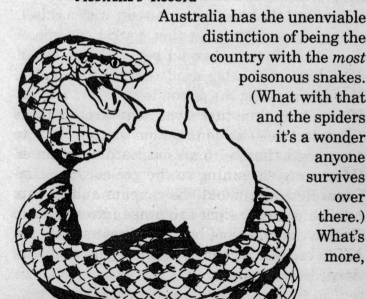

Australia has the unenviable distinction of being the country with the *most* poisonous snakes. (What with that and the spiders it's a wonder anyone survives over there.) What's more,

Australia is home to nine of the world's top ten poisonous snakes.

The Terrible Taipan

One of them is the taipan, found mainly in north Queensland. The taipan is distinguished by a set of particularly long fangs so it can plunge its venom deep inside you. For years very few people ever survived a taipan bite. One man who did was bitten through a leather boot, which provided some protection. His friends pulled the boot off and gashed the bite area repeatedly with a chisel, producing deep bleeding that got rid of some of the poison. A four-year-old boy who was bitten six times on the leg died ten minutes later. That's how strong the poison is.

For a long time there was no protection from a taipan bite – no anti-venom existed. It was discovered thanks to an extraordinary act of heroism by a young snake collector called Kevin Budden. In 1950 he caught a taipan in a rubbish tip. As he tried to put it into a sack, it bit him several times on the thumb. With the deadly poison already spreading through his veins, Kevin insisted that the snake should be sent to the Serum Laboratories in Melbourne.

A few hours later Kevin was dead. The snake was sent to the Melbourne Laboratories and its venom extracted. After years of research an anti-venom for taipan bites was finally produced.

The Deadly Brown Snake

Another deadly Australian species is the brown snake. Its poison is reckoned to be the second most powerful in the world. One evening in December 1991 some friends were sitting on the banks of the Murray River when they saw a swimming snake. Rashly, one of them jumped in, swam after it, and seized hold of it. As he took it back to the bank it bit him on the hand.

Returning to the bank the angry swimmer killed the snake. His worried friends called for an ambulance and he was taken to hospital but his heart stopped and he died on the way. The snake turned out to be a brown snake. The man had died just over half an hour after being bitten.

About 3000 Australians are bitten by poisonous snakes every year – but thanks to the development and availability of anti-venom, deaths from snakebite are the exception today. Between 1981 and 1991 only 18 deaths from snakebite were reported to the Melbourne Laboratories.

Top Killer

Winner of the competition for most dangerous snake is the saw-scaled or carpet viper. Found in West Africa, the Middle East and India, it's reckoned to have bitten and killed more people than any other snake in the world. It's believed to kill 80 000 people a year in Asia alone. What makes the carpet viper so dangerous? Its small, and easily overlooked – until it's too late. It's venom is highly poisonous – more than most other snakes. Above all, it's extremely bad-tempered. Many snakes are shy and will slither away if they get the chance. Not the carpet viper. Annoy or even disturb it and it turns very nasty . . .

Fast Mover

The fastest snake in the world is the dreaded, and extremely venomous black mamba, found mainly in East Africa. There are stories that it can catch up with a man on horseback, but that's probably an exaggeration. However, it has been timed at 10-12 miles an hour over a short stretch – enough to make the fittest of athletes run for his life.

Bushmaster

Another very dangerous snake is the bush

master, found in the jungles of Central America. The famous explorer, Colonel Fawcett, had a nasty encounter with one in Bolivia in 1907. "All of a sudden, something made me jump sideways and open my legs wide. Between them shot the wicked head and huge body of a striking bushmaster." Talk about a close shave – it makes you wince to think of it! (Then again, Colonel Fawcett once claimed to have shot a 62-foot-long anaconda. Maybe some of his stories need a pinch of salt.)

The bushmaster is one of the largest poisonous snakes in the world, often reaching a length of 12 feet. The best thing about it is that you're highly unlikely to bump into it. It lives in the depths of the jungle and meets very few people. In Costa Rica, only 10 people have been recorded as being bitten by bushmasters. (Mind you, five of them died.)

An interesting thing about the bushmaster is that it has its own built-in sensor-system. Heat-sensitive pits on either side of its nose enable it to detect possible prey with amazing accuracy.

A Question of Size

Poisonous snakes come in all sizes, but some kinds of non-poisonous snakes depend on their

size and strength. Unpleasant as it is to think of snake-venom spreading through your veins, it's almost as nasty to imagine yourself in the affectionate embrace of a python.

The biggest snake in the world is the South American anaconda. The largest recorded so far was shot in Brazil in 1960. It was nearly 28 feet long, 44 inches in diameter and weighed about 500 pounds. The python can grow even longer, but is rather more slimline.

Pythons, and the other "constrictor" snakes, kill by suffocation, compressing their victim's chest till it can longer breathe. Once their prey is dead, or at least unconscious, the big snake begins its meal. Since snakes can't chew they have to swallow their food whole. To do this they're equipped with expanding jaws. When swallowing something extra bulky, the bones in their jaws and even in their skulls can move apart.

African rock pythons will regularly swallow quite large deer, and there are stories of them swallowing people, though these have been mostly babies or small children. In 1972 a young boy was swallowed by a 20-foot python in Burma. Angry villagers got their own back by eating the snake. However, there are some accounts of snakes swallowing fully-grown men. In 1927 some Burmese hunters, looking for a missing member of their party, found an extremely full python with the man's hat and shoes beside it. They killed the python, cut it open and found the missing hunter dead inside

Another such instance occurred in South Africa in 1979. An unfortunate young herdsman of the Tswana tribe was guarding his cattle when he was seized by a 14-foot African rock python which started to swallow him. His terrified friend ran to fetch help, returning twenty minutes later with a couple of men. By this time the young herdsman was completely inside the snake. Bravely the two men attacked the snake with stones and a pickaxe, and the angry snake regurgitated its prey. Sadly, the young man was already dead – killed perhaps, by sheer fright.

Spitting Snakes
You might think you were safe as long as you kept well away from snakes but it's not always so. Some cobras can rear up and spit their poison – as far as 9 feet! The poison is usually aimed at the eyes and can cause temporary, or even permanent blindness.

Snake Statistics
According to the World Health Organization over 30 000 people a year die from snakebite. That's all over the world, though. If you live in Great Britain, you really don't need to worry – well, not much anyway.

We've already mentioned Britain's only poisonous snake, the adder. It's pretty rare and extremely shy. Unless you actually sit on one, you're probably pretty safe. Moreover, its bite isn't necessarily fatal. (A depressed business man once tried to commit suicide by letting an adder bite him. He lost his arm, but not his life.) Over the last fifty years, there have been 7 deaths from snakebite in Britain.

Jaws!

Horror films are most successful when they reflect our fears. Steven Spielberg struck just such a chord with his film *Jaws*. Based on a novel by Peter Benchley, the film tells of the hunt for a shark which is terrorizing a Long Island beach resort. *Jaws* was made in 1975, over twenty years ago – but the memory can still give you a nasty twinge when you try sea-bathing.

Benchley and Spielberg had hit upon a basic truth. For humans the sea is a dangerous alien environment. When we swim in it, most of us hangs under the surface, unprotected. The thought of something surging up and snapping at our dangly bits is extremely upsetting.

It's particularly unpleasant if that something might be a shark. The creature's whole image is peculiarly terrifying. The streamlined head, the rows of teeth, the cold black eyes . . .

The shark is a basic killing machine, a primitive creature that has roamed the seas for 350 million years.

It's true to say that, just as with snakes and spiders, our fears about sharks are exaggerated – hyped up in a way by *Jaws* and other movies. Indignant naturalists tell us that the shark isn't as savage as it's made out to be, and that we attack sharks far more than sharks attack us. (If you consider the popularity of the macho sport of shark-fishing, this may well be true.) But just as with the spider and the snake, the danger does exist. There's no doubt that shark attacks do happen. Sharks kill about 50 people a year. So how dangerous is the shark?

An Early Jaws

A series of events that might almost have inspired Peter Benchley's best-seller occurred off the New Jersey coast in 1916. It was 1 July, in a little resort called Beech Haven, and a young man called Charles Van Sant had just arrived on holiday.

Not wanting to waste a single moment, he changed into swimming things, left his family at the hotel and went to the beach, dashing straight into the sea. Young and strong and a

good swimmer, he went quite a way out, before turning and swimming back to shore.

Suddenly a black fin appeared in the water behind him. People on the beach saw it and shouted warnings but Charles didn't hear. When he was quite close to the beach there was a sudden flurry and the sea around him turned red . . . An Olympic swimmer called Ott was on the beach. He plunged bravely in and swam out to help Charles. As he approached, a grey shape slid away. Ott managed to get Charles to shore, where he saw that both legs had been savagely mangled. Charles died that evening, from shock and from loss of blood.

The incident caused some alarm, but it was seen as a one-off freak attack. There was no record of a shark attacking a bather in the area before.

Five days later, with the beach still crowded, a young Swiss called Charles Bruder, a bellboy from one of the local hotels, went in for a swim on his day off. It was low tide, so he walked out till the water was waist high and started to swim. Suddenly a woman screamed as the sea around Bruder turned red with blood. Two men launched a boat and rowed out to help. As they hauled him from the bloody water, he gasped, "A shark's had both my legs. . ." Bruder died almost immediately. The post mortem established that his right leg and left foot had been torn off. The second attack provoked panic, and motor boats filled with men armed with rifles and spotlights patrolled the shoreline for several nights. Not a single shark was seen.

On 12 July some children were swimming in the creek at a little town called Matawan, several miles inland. A black shape surged up and seized a child called Lester, dragging him under the water. The children's screams attracted help and a young man called Stanley Fisher dived in to search for Lester's body. He dived, but didn't return to the surface. There was a sudden flurry and a spreading cloud of blood. Suddenly Fisher reappeared – clutching the remains of one of his own legs. He was pulled to shore and taken to the hospital, where he died on the operating table.

Further up the creek more children were swimming from a dock. When they heard what was happening, they left the water in a rush. Joseph Dunne, the youngest, was the last to leave the water. Half-way up the ladder, something seized his right leg. His brother and his friends grabbed him, heaving in a gruesome tug-of-war until the shark released its hold.

Joseph survived the attack, although he lost his leg. The shark had attacked three times in less than an hour.

This series of attacks provoked panic on a massive scale and a huge shark hunt was launched. The creek was blocked with metal nets, and dynamite was set off in all likely spots. No shark was found, but Lester's body was recovered near the spot where he had disappeared. There were seven bite marks on the body.

Two days later, a fisherman caught a huge shark just off South Amboy. Opening it up he found it full of human remains – including a piece of bone later identified as being from Charles Bruder's leg. Since there were no more attacks after this it seems likely that the shark, identified as a Great White, was responsible for all of them.

Shark Beach

South of Durban, in South Africa, Amanzimtoti Beach stretches out from the rolling sand dunes. The place is a popular holiday resort and the surrounding sea is very full of swimmers and surfers – and sometimes sharks . . .

Amanzimtoti Beach is top of the league tables for shark attacks. Four attacks took place in one year alone. On 7 January 1974, a young man called Cornelius was bathing with hundreds of other swimmers in the same stretch of water. What they didn't realize was that floods from a local river had broken down some of the off-shore shark nets.

Suddenly something bumped Cornelius out of the water and he realized that it must be a shark. Yelling an alarm he punched at it and swam for the beach. Some surfers came to his aid, helping him to reach the shore. His legs were badly gashed but that was all. He was taken to hospital where he made a good recovery.

On 14 February the shark nets were still damaged, and bathing was forbidden. John Kendrick and his friend Joe defied the ban because Kendrick was keen to train for the lifesaving championships. It nearly cost him his own.

As they were swimming Joe suddenly felt something bump against him. He yelled a warning to Kendrick to swim for the shore. Kendrick turned to see what was the matter – and felt teeth close round his leg. The shark started shaking him to and fro. Kendrick said later that everything had happened so fast that he didn't realize what was going on. Seconds later the shark released him and he was caught by the breakers and thrown up on the sand. Bleeding heavily he staggered up the beach.

It wasn't until he looked down that he realised that the whole calf of his leg had been bitten away. Someone on the beach knew enough to put on a tourniquet, undoubtedly saving Kendrick's life. He had been bitten not once but three times, and his leg had to be amputated below the knee.

Absence of initial pain, and so not realizing the extent of the injury, is an odd feature common to many shark attacks. It has even been suggested the shark produces some kind of anaesthetic. What's far more likely is that the shark attacks with such incredible force that the victim is numbed with shock.

On 21 March 1974, a young surfer called James Gurr was breaking the beach rules by surfing after 4 p.m. The ban had been imposed after the earlier attacks – sharks were thought to be more dangerous later in the day. Suddenly James saw a shark's fin zooming towards him. The impact knocked him off his board. He was still fastened by a line and he scrambled to get back on. A huge chunk had been bitten from his surfboard.

James managed to get back on the board, lying on his back with his feet up. Another heavy impact knocked him off again. As he swam for the board, he actually felt the body of the shark against his side. Scrambling on the board again, he started paddling frantically for the shore.

A third terrific jolt knocked him face down in the water. He got back on the board again and paddled for the shore again – with the shark zigzagging ahead of him! As he reached the shore, a huge breaking wave threw him off the board, right over the shark, and back on to the sand. The breakers caught his body and swept him back to the shore. Astonishingly, he was unhurt – only the board had been bitten.

On 4 April, a young lad called Anthony was wind-surfing with his brother offshore. He was wearing a white sock on his right foot, which was in the strap of the surfboard. Suddenly Anthony felt something tug at his foot. Realizing it was a shark he looked down "to see if my legs were still there". They were – but his white sock was red with blood. Anthony and his brother paddled rapidly to shore where Anthony found a great gash along

his heel. It needed nineteen stitches – but he was glad to have got off so lightly.

Ten months later, on 23 February 1975, Russel Jones was surfing with two friends. He was sitting on his board dangling his feet in the water when something bumped his right foot – which was covered in a bright yellow sock. Thinking it was a rock he started to pull his legs up – and then felt something clamp around his right foot "like the jaws of a steel trap".

Yelling the alarm, Russel tried desperately to pull his leg from the water. Suddenly it came free and he began paddling frantically to the shore. He felt no pain until he reached the sand – and tried to walk on the stump of his right leg. . .

His foot had been bitten off, just above the ankle. In each case, it seems likely that the bright, light socks attracted the shark.

Sharks and Shipwrecks

Shipwrecks seem to be made to order for sharks. They are attracted by noise and by vibration – and above all, by blood. Sharks can detect food traces in the water to a ratio of one in ten *billion*. It's reckoned that there are around 50 000 shipwreck victims around the world every year. Those unlucky enough to be wrecked in dangerous waters, will often have to face the extra danger of sharks.

The *Nova Scotia* – 1942

The worst shark attack so far recorded happened in the Indian Ocean during the Second World War. The English steamer *Nova Scotia* was 30 miles off the South African coast, en route for Durban. The ship was crowded with men. As well as her regular crew, the *Nova Scotia* was carrying 765 Italian prisoners of war and 134 South African soldiers.

On the morning of 18 November 1942, the *Nova Scotia* encountered a German submarine, which fired a salvo of torpedoes. The ship sank almost at once, and over nine hundred men were thrown into the sea. The ship's lifeboats had caught fire during the attack and most of the survivors were floating in life jackets, or clinging to life-rafts and pieces of debris. Soon the sharks began to gather.

One of the shipwrecked soldiers tells how he was clinging to a spar with another man from his regiment: "Suddenly he screamed and the entire top half of his body was literally lifted out of the water. When he fell back again the sea was covered with blood and I saw that his foot had been severed. At this point I caught sight of the grey form of a shark swimming excitedly around us."

All around similar scenes must have been taking place – but very few of the sharks' victims survived to tell the tale. The survivor of this particular attack swam away as fast as he could, and was fortunate enough to find a floating life-raft. He and some other survivors scrambled aboard, and waited for rescue. Sharks circled around their raft all the time. Often they had to beat them off with oars.

Together with others less fortunate, they were in the water for 67 hours before being rescued by a Portuguese sloop. As the rescuers started picking up survivors, sharks lunged at them out of the water. The Portuguese sailors had to beat off hordes of them with boathooks.

Altogether 194 survivors were rescued. 700 men died in the shipwreck. Some of course would have been killed or wounded in the initial attack, and others must have drowned. However, the sea was warm and the men were young and fit, likely to survive long enough to be rescued. It seems certain that most of the 700 missing fell victim to the sharks.

Una – 1918

Another tragic shipwreck occurred in 1918, at the end of the First World War. The steamer *Una* struck a sandbank, just off Santo Domingo in the Caribbean Sea. There was a shortage of lifeboats and the few that were available were promptly collared by the captain and his officers. The 75 sailors had to make do with very basic wooden life-rafts – and there weren't even enough of those. As the overcrowded life-rafts bobbed towards shore the sharks began to gather. Some of the rafts were so overloaded that men fell off – and were immediately snapped up by the sharks. As time went on the sharks became more and more aggressive.

They would lash the rafts with their tails to try and overturn them, or bump them from underneath to throw the men off. Sometimes a shark would simply rear out of the water, rest its head on the raft, and seize its victim by an arm or leg, dragging him into the sea. Only a handful of the 75 sailors reached the shore alive.

The *Dona Paz* – 1987

The wreck of the *Dona Paz* is exceptionally horrifying, not only because of the large number of passengers involved, but because there were almost no survivors.

The ferry boat that eventually became the *Dona Paz* was originally built in Japan in the sixties. It was licensed to carry 600 passengers. After years of service, it was sold off to a ferry company in the Philippine Islands. It was reconditioned, and its official passenger load was raised to 1500.

As Christmas approaches, Philippine islanders travel extensively from island to island, visiting family and friends. As long as they get there, they don't much mind how crowded their transport is, and regulations are relaxed even more than usual. It is estimated that between three and four *thousand* passengers were packed onto the *Dona Paz* when she sailed from Manila on 20 December 1987.

At ten o'clock that night an oil tanker called the *Victor* collided with the *Dona Paz*. The tanker was loaded with barrels of oil which immediately caught fire and exploded. The fire spread from one ship to the other and the sea around the two ships was covered with blazing oil. Even viewed simply as a shipwreck this was a catastrophe. The combination of the fire and the terrible overcrowding of the vessel meant that safety procedures were non-existent. No lifeboats were launched and many died before they could swim away from the burning sea.

What adds the final touch of horror is that the China Seas are particularly rich in sharks – the Great White, the Tiger shark, the Blue shark, and many more. Moreover, the shipwreck had everything to attract them – the noise of the explosions, the screams of the victims and, above all, the blood of the wounded in the water. And the sharks certainly came.

As news of the catastrophe spread, rescuers sped to the scene in boats and helicopters.

They found hardly anybody left alive. Of the three or four thousand passengers only two women and 23 men were rescued. Hundreds of mangled corpses were found floating in the water for miles around. For weeks afterwards, Philippine fishermen found human remains in the stomachs of the sharks they caught.

A Terrible Trio

So there you are then – a few frightening facts about a terrible trio, spiders, snakes and sharks. Don't let them worry you too much. There are no poisonous spiders in England – or rather, since all spiders are poisonous really, none with poison strong enough to do you any harm. Our snakes are harmless too, as long as you avoid the adder. Whatever the hazards of English beaches, they don't include the Great White shark. And if you ever go to South Africa and fancy a swim on a hot sunny day – well, you can always avoid Amanzimtoti Beach.

TERRORIST HORROR

Horrific as some members of the animal kingdom can be, there can be no doubt about the most dangerous creature on our planet: man. We are said to be the only animal that kills for sport and fights its own species to the death over matters not related to survival. Amongst humans, one of the most dangerous types is the terrorist – someone whose belief in a cause is so strong that he or she is prepared to commit almost any atrocity if it will further the cause.

However different their political beliefs – from the Communist Red Brigade to the Neo-Nazis – terrorists all tend to use the same methods – hostage-taking and the bomb. The bomb that kills or maims men, women and children indiscriminately. The hostage, who is threatened and sometimes killed – simply for being in the wrong place at the wrong time. Bombs and hostages make news, and terrorists crave above all what politicians call "the oxygen of publicity".

What makes terrorists so frightening is their complete absence of conscience or remorse. They follow the fearful logic of the terrifying Jesuit belief: "If the end be good, the means are also good." Or to give the modern version, "The end justifies the means". Terrorists believe, indeed they know, that they are *right* – that the evil they do will be justified by some

future good. It reminds you of another old saying: "The road to hell is paved with good intentions"...

The Exiles

One particularly hard-line terrorist group originated in Palestine. The creation of Israel in 1948
made Palestinians feel that they had lost their
homeland. Refugees fled into nearby Jordan and
Syria. There, in the territory of sympathetic fel-
low-Arab governments the "Intifada" began – a
holy crusade whose objectives were the destruction of Israel and the establishment of an inde-
pendent Palestinian state.

There is no doubt that the Palestinians had
genuine grievances. They chose to bring them
to the world's attention by a campaign of ruthless terrorism. In 1970 there were a number of
airliner hijackings. Then, in 1972, during the
Munich Olympics, there occurred one of the
worst outrages of all.

It started at 5 a.m. on the morning of 2 May
1972. An early-bird telephone engineer, working near the Olympic village, saw a group of
men in casual sports clothes, carrying sports
bags, climbing over the 7-foot perimeter fence.
The engineer assumed they were athletes,

sneaking back after a night on the town, and he didn't report them. It was a terrible mistake. Less than an hour later, the four men, hooded and carrying automatic weapons that had been concealed in their bags burst into a room in Block 31 – the quarters of the Israeli team.

They opened fire with Kalashnikov rifles, wounding two Israeli athletes lying on their beds. For a while everything was in confusion. Warned by the gunshots, some of the athletes in nearby rooms were able to get away.

Two Israeli athletes were killed trying to escape. Tuvia Sokolovsky, a weightlifting coach, actually did manage to escape, zigzagging to avoid the terrorists' bullets. The German authorities reacted swiftly. The building was surrounded by German police and Olympic security guards. Marksmen were placed in position on nearby roofs. When the situation became clear, it emerged that the besieged terrorists were holding nine Israeli athletes hostage. The terrorists, members of the Palestinian Black September group, issued their demands: 230 Palestinian Arab prisoners, held in Israel, were to be released. Failing this, one hostage would be executed every two hours. The executions would begin at noon.

When these terms were conveyed to Golda Meir, then Israeli Prime Minister, her response was uncompromising. No prisoners would be released. The Israelis, knowing themselves to be targets of terrorist attack, had determined on a hard-line policy from the beginning. No surrender to terrorist demands – ever.

The terrorists' midday deadline passed. There were no executions. Negotiations continued. Second, third and fourth deadlines were set — and still there were no executions.

By now the Olympic village was sealed off from the world. Behind the scenes, more furious negotiations were going on. The terrorists, convinced by now that the Israelis meant what they said, offered a different deal. The safety of the hostages, in return for their own freedom. The German authorities agreed.

It was decided that Egypt should act as go-between in the deal. A plan was hammered out: terrorists and hostages would be taken to a nearby military airfield, there they would all board a Lufthansa Boeing 707, which would take them to Cairo. From there, the Egyptians guaranteed the safe return of the hostages.

At 8.30 p.m. three helicopters landed in the grounds of the Olympic village. As arranged, they flew the terrorists and their hostages to the airfield where the Lufthansa plane was waiting, surrounded by armed German security forces. Soon after the helicopters landed, shooting broke out. In the swift and bloody gun battle that followed, all nine Israeli hostages were killed — together with four terrorists, a helicopter pilot and a policeman. Three more terrorists were captured trying to escape from the field.

In the charges and counter-charges that followed the disaster, it was hard to make out what had actually happened. It seems that the German security forces had lost faith in the Egyptian promise to return the hostages, and had decided on a last-minute rescue attempt. The transfer to the aircraft seemed to offer the only opportunity. But it had all gone wrong . . .

As in all cases of hostage-taking, the authorities faced a terrible dilemma – damned if they acted, equally damned if they held back.

A terrorist incident over ten years later, also involving Palestinian guerrillas, had a very different result.

The Achille Lauro - 1985

On 8 October 1985, the *Achille Lauro* arrived at Alexandria from Genoa, her home port. The *Achille Lauro* was an old Dutch freighter, bought by an Italian company and converted into a cruise liner.

The *Achille Lauro* had arrived at 7.30 a.m. and put ashore over 600 of her passengers. As an optional part of the cruise, these passengers were to travel overland to Cairo. When they'd seen the pyramids and some of the other sights of Egypt they would proceed to Port Said where the *Achille Lauro* would pick them up. These 600 passengers didn't yet know it, but opting for the Cairo trip was the luckiest decision they'd ever made.

The *Achille Lauro* then set sail for Port Said. She carried a crew of 330, and the remaining 180 passengers who had decided to stay with the ship.

When the *Achille Lauro* was about 30 miles away from Alexandria, Palestinian gunmen appeared. Terrifying passengers and crew by spraying bullets everywhere, they seized control of the bridge, and then of the rest of the ship. Astonishingly, there were only four of them. Four desperate men armed with automatic weapons who were quite prepared to kill – as they later proved. Their leader. Mohammed Abbas, known as Abul, told the *Achille Lauro*'s captain, Captain de Rosa, that his ship was now in the hands of the PLF – the Palestinian Liberation Front. He would be well advised to cooperate fully, or he would be responsible for any harm that came to his passengers. (This by the way, is a fairly typical terrorist attitude. If you don't do as they say and they're forced to kill you, then of course it's all *your* fault for being difficult.)

At 9.45 p.m. the Egyptian authorities received a radio message from Captain de Rosa. He told them that his ship was in

the hands of an armed force of Palestinian terrorists. They were demanding the freeing of
fifty fellow-terrorists, held prisoner by Israel.

If their demands were not met, or if any
attempt was made to recapture the ship, the
Achille Lauro would be blown up.

The *Achille Lauro* sailed away out of radio
range – leaving the Egyptian government in a
considerable dilemma. Egypt, of course was
an Arab nation, in sympathy with the
Palestinians rather than with the Israelis. But
Egypt was also on good terms with the West.
What's more, she wanted things to stay that
way.

Egypt informed the Italian and Israeli governments of what had happened. Egyptian officials got a copy of the passenger list and
informed the respective governments of the
passengers involved. It was a very mixed bag.
The crew were mainly Italian, but included
some Portuguese and also some British. The
passenger list showed 28 Italians, 52 Swiss, 3
British, 16 Americans, 22 Germans and
Austrians, and 11 Belgians. In addition to
Egypt, seven different national governments
were involved in the *Achille Lauro* affair.

On board the *Achille Lauro* the situation
was grim. In some instances hijackers have
been known to try to build good relations with

their victims. This sometimes results in something known as the "Stockholm syndrome" — after a Swedish siege in which a bond of sympathy grew up between kidnappers and hostages.

Nothing like this happened on board the *Achille Lauro*. On the contrary, the guerrillas went out of their way to treat their captives as harshly as possible. They insulted them, and abused them, and threatened them with death. Either they would die together when the *Achille Lauro* was blown up, or one by one, when the terrorists began selective executions.

British and American captives were particularly badly treated. They were separated from the rest and surrounded with cans of petrol — to be set alight on any rescue attempt.

One of the passengers was a Mr Klinghoffer, an elderly Jewish man from New York. Despite the fact that he was confined to a wheelchair, Mr Klinghoffer wasn't afraid to speak his mind. He told his captors exactly what he thought of them and their barbaric behaviour. However much he was threatened, he still refused to shut up. Fearing he might encourage other captives to rebel, the guerrillas dragged him from his chair on to the open deck. They shot him twice in the back, and dumped his body into the sea.

By now the *Achille Lauro* was off the coast of Syria, and the terrorists used the radio to issue further demands. They wanted a Red Cross ship to bring the Ambassadors of America, Germany, Italy and Britain to negotiate with them. They also wanted a meeting with a delegation from the Arab Liberation Front.

Syria ignored their demands. Suspected in the past of involvement with and support of terrorist groups, Syria, like Egypt, wanted to clean up its image in the West. Backing piracy and terrorism wasn't the way to do it.

Turned away where they'd expected help and support, the terrorists made Captain de Rosa take the *Achille Lauro* back to Port Said. The Egyptians refused to allow the ship to enter port.

In response, the guerillas renewed their threats to blow up the ship – and demanded to meet the Ambassadors of America, Germany, Italy and Britain. Now the attention of the world was focused on Egypt. Reluctant as they were to be involved, the Egyptians thought they'd better start some sort of negotiation.

The ship was allowed to anchor offshore, and an Egyptian naval vessel brought out a mixed party of Red Cross representatives, Italian officials, Egyptian officials, and a delegation from the Palestinian Liberation Organization.

By now the guerrillas had realized that their demands weren't going to be met. They were willing to settle for a lot less. After several hours of negotiation, the Egyptian authorities announced that the siege of the *Achille Lauro* would end at 5 p.m. with the surrender of the gunmen. On the morning of 10 October the *Achille Lauro* docked, and the released hostages came ashore.

The Egyptian government had done a deal – the release of the hostages, in return for safe passage from Egypt for the terrorists. It must have seemed like the simplest way out of a tricky situation, and it had certainly saved the lives of the hostages – all but one, who it was too late to save.

Because of that one missing hostage the trouble wasn't over. The released hostages were telling their story now, and a storm of indignation swept America over the murder of Mr Klinghoffer.

That indignation turned against the Egyptian government when the truth leaked out – the terrorists were to be released unpunished.

The Egyptians did their best to stall. First they said that they'd agreed to the release of the terrorists before they knew about Mr Klinghoffer's murder. Nobody believed them. The Egyptians then tried to suggest that the released hostages' story was exaggerated. After all, Mr Klinghoffer had been old and frail. Perhaps he'd died of natural causes . . . This story lost all credibility when Leon Klinghoffer's body was washed ashore – with two bullets in the back.

Meanwhile the four terrorists had been quietly taken to Cairo Airport, where they were put on board an Egyptian Boeing 737 to Tunis, their chosen destination.

The Americans decided they weren't going to let them get away with murder. Four American fighters intercepted the Egyptian Boeing 747 and forced it to land at a Nato air base in Sicily.

What happened next was a diplomatic and military farce. Armed Italian police surrounded the Egyptian Boeing, surrounding them was a cordon of US Marines. Instead of uniting to deal with the terrorists, the two countries were confronting each other! Much as one can sympathize with their prompt and daring action, the Americans had ignored diplomatic custom and international law. The Italians were furious.

Italy insisted that since the crimes had taken place on an Italian vessel, the terrorists must be tried in Italian courts. The Egyptians gave the Italians their full support. They deplored the hijacking of the *Achille Lauro* – but they equally deplored the American hijacking of their Boeing 737! Since the law was on their side, the Italians eventually won. The terrorists were released into Italian custody, and the Americans applied for their extradition.

The results were everything the Americans had feared. Somehow, during the long, legal wrangling, the terrorists mysteriously slipped away to Belgrade. The Italians said they had been held "without motive, and longer than necessary".

The resulting scandal brought down the Italian government. It was small consolation to the Americans, and to the relatives of Leon Klinghoffer – the brave old man who defied the terrorists from his wheelchair and paid with his life.

Terrorism in London

Not all terrorist attacks take place in exotic places. Some of the most dramatic have occurred in London. . .

The Balcombe Street Siege - 1975

In the winter of 1975 there was a sudden upsurge in IRA (Irish Republican Army) activity in London. Incendiary bombs were planted in shops, and gunmen opened fire on West End restaurants. In November, author and journalist Ross McWhirter, who had been leading a campaign against the IRA, was shot dead on his own doorstep.

The police were convinced that a ruthless and very active IRA cell was at large in London. Based on their experience of previous incidents, they reckoned that the gang's next step would be to steal a car to carry out their next attack.

The streets of London were flooded with armed detectives, and a hot line was set up to give them immediate news of stolen cars. On the evening of Saturday 6 December, a blue Ford Cortina was stolen in Notting Hill. Its description was broadcast, and soon it was picked up in Mayfair by an unmarked police car. Sending out a radio alert, the police car followed the Cortina, which was moving suspiciously slowly. As the Cortina passed Scotts Restaurant, a volley of shots was fired and the blue car sped away.

The police car gave chase, and was soon joined by a yellow Cortina from the Flying Squad and a Special Patrol Group van. As the little convoy raced through the West End, the men in the blue Cortina fired several shots at their pursuers.

The car was abandoned in Marylebone and four men were seen running away. The chase continued on foot, with police and gunmen exchanging shots.

By now the area was ringed by armed police, and the fleeing men were surrounded close to Marylebone Station. As the police closed in, the men dashed into the open doorway of a block of flats in Balcombe Street. They ran up to the first floor and forced their way into an apartment, taking hostage the two people inside. The flat was occupied by a middle-aged couple, Post Office Inspector John Matthews, and his wife Sheila. For them it was all like a nightmare. They'd been having a quiet evening at home – and suddenly their flat was full of armed men yelling threats!

Three of the four men, Duggan, O'Connell and Butler, came from Ireland. The fourth, Doherty, came from Glasgow. All four were in their twenties. The four men and their two hostages were barricaded in the front room of the flat. The police had followed the men into the flat and occupied all the rooms around. Sir Robert Mark, the then Commissioner of the Metropolitan Police, took charge of the siege. A field telephone was passed into the room, so that police and terrorists could talk.

In a strong Irish accent, one of the terrorists conveyed their demands. They wanted safe conduct, a car to Heathrow, and air-travel back to Ireland – on an Irish plane. In the short term, they wanted food and water. Unless all demands were met, both hostages would be killed. Sir Robert Mark rejected most of the demands. The terrorists were given some water – and a portable chemical toilet. . .

The siege settled down into the usual stalemate. The Police Commissioner said that as far as he was concerned the besieged men were ordinary criminals. All they could expect was a fair trial. His main concern, he said, was to avoid bloodshed. "We are prepared to surround this flat until these people see reason."

The siege was to drag on for almost a week. During this time, relations between police and terrorists went through various ups and downs. A Home Office psychologist had advised Sir Robert Mark not to be *too* hard-line, to leave the terrorists at least the hope of making some kind of deal.

Some soup was offered for Mrs Matthews. Angrily, the terrorists turned it down. A few days later, however, food was offered and accepted. Negotiations were begun about the possible release of Mrs Matthews, in exchange for more food. The police had been allowed to talk to her on the telephone. Although she had said bravely they were "doing all right", it was obvious from her voice that she was under enormous strain.

Towards the end of the week things suddenly took a turn for the worse. After screaming abuse down the telephone, the gunmen threw the food they had been given out of the window. They threw the field telephone out as well.

In response the police cut off the electricity. The flat was plunged into darkness – and the terrorists could no longer watch themselves on the news on the Matthews' television.

Detective-Superintendent Imbert, who was in charge on the ground, felt that the siege was now at its critical stage. In an effort to reduce the tension, and the risk to the hostages, he offered the terrorists hot coffee and cigarettes. The offer was refused. Next day, however, on Friday the 12th, the atmosphere improved. Food and drink were offered again, and accepted.

Then came the first real breakthrough in the siege. Suddenly Mrs Matthews appeared on the balcony outside the flat. She was escorted by a hooded, but apparently unarmed terrorist. Police beckoned her forward and she was allowed to move along the balcony and into the next flat. One of the hostages was free!

From now on it was only a matter of time. More food was sent into the flat and the field telephone was replaced. The terrorists had long discussions with Superintendent Imbert. More food was sent in and the four terrorists and Mr Matthews had a meal together.

There was more talk on the telephone and

then, at about 4.25 p.m., all four terrorists walked out of the flat and surrendered. The Balcombe Street Siege was over. Although worn out by continuous tension, and by the lack of food and sleep, Mr and Mrs Matthews came through it without serious harm. After some time in hospital, both made a good recovery.

If the demands of the terrorists are denied – and they almost invariably are – the authorities in a hostage situation face some difficult decisions. They can wait things out, trying to keep negotiations going, until the terrorists see things are hopeless and surrender. Or they can attack, risking the lives of the hostages. What you might call the soft and hard approaches.

In the case of the *Achille Lauro* the soft

approach saved all but one of the hostages, but the terrorists escaped. At Munich, the hard approach got all the hostages, as well as some of the terrorists, killed. Generally speaking, the soft approach, as exemplified by the Balcombe Street siege, has the highest success rate. But there are exceptions.

Nightmare at Entebbe – 1976

The Air France plane left Tel Aviv for Paris at 9 a.m. on 27 June 1976. Soon after the plane took off four passengers produced revolvers and left their seats.

One, a young woman, covered the first-class passengers. Two others, dark-skinned, Arab-looking men, took over the larger, more crowded tourist section. The fourth man, who was fair-haired and European, forced his way into the cockpit. He had a revolver in one hand and a grenade in the other.

Later, the identities, or at least the aliases, of the four terrorists were discovered from the passenger lists. The young woman's name was Ortega, and she came from Ecuador. The two Arabs came from Kuwait and from Bahrain. The blond man, the leader, was registered as a Peruvian called Garcia. In actual fact he was German – his name was Boese.

Soon afterwards, all air-to-ground radio contact was lost.

The Air France plane had vanished.

The missing plane reappeared close to Benghazi Airport in Libya at about 2 p.m. The captain, following the hijackers' instructions, asked for fuel for a four-hour onward flight. He also asked for a meeting with the local

representative of the PFLP – the Popular Front for the Liberation of Palestine.

The Libyans allowed the plane to land on a remote runway. Here one enterprising young woman actually managed to talk her way off the plane. She told the terrorists that she was pregnant – which was obviously true. She also told them that she had a long history of medical complications, and would certainly have a miscarriage if she was forced to remain on board. Not wishing to have to cope with medical emergencies, the terrorists let her go. (In fact, while the pregnancy was genuine, the complications were a complete invention.) The mother-to-be continued her journey to England. For her fellow passengers, a long nightmare was just beginning.

The plane was kept waiting on the runway in Benghazi for seven hours – with the hostages in ever-increasing terror for their lives. Suddenly refuelling began and soon afterwards the plane took off again.

News of the hijacked plane had spread all over the world by now, and everyone waited to see what its next destination would be.

After a long flight, with its fuel almost exhausted, the plane landed at Entebbe, in Uganda. At the time the country was under the military dictatorship of the infamous

General Idi Amin.

By now the usual diplomatic discussions were under way. Since it was a French plane, France felt responsible for the safety of the plane and its passengers.

The Israelis were pretty sure that they were the ones under attack. There were 246 passengers on board. Of these, 145 were Jewish. Of the 145 Jews, 77 were Israeli citizens. The Israelis felt that these Jewish passengers were the real targets of the hijack. Events were to prove them right.

There was something uniquely dangerous about this particular hijack. The terrorists had managed to take refuge in an *openly* friendly country. If only for the sake of international relations, most countries are reluctant to be seen publicly supporting terrorism – however sympathetic they feel to the terrorist cause. General Amin, however, had little or no interest in international co-operation. He had recently severed diplomatic relations with Israel, and he had frequently been known to speak favourably of the PLO. Looking out of the plane, passengers could see the terrorists talking to Ugandan soldiers. They were obviously on the friendliest of terms.

At midday the passengers were taken from the plane. Guarded by Ugandan soldiers, they were moved to the airport's terminal buildings, and held there under guard. Meanwhile the terrorists were issuing their demands to the rest of the world.

To nobody's surprise, the hijack had been carried out by the PFLP – the Popular Front for the Liberation of Palestine. They were demanding the release of over fifty terrorist prisoners, held not only in Israel, but in Germany, France, Switzerland and Kenya as well. If their demands were not met, the terrorists would blow up the plane. (At this point no one knew the prisoners had already been moved.)

Conditions inside the old air terminal buildings were cramped and uncomfortable, and facilities primitive. On the pretext of giving the prisoners more room, Ugandan soldiers knocked a hole in the wall to the next room.

Suddenly Boese, the blond-haired German terrorist, appeared with a complete passenger list. He began calling out names from the list. Passengers called had to move through the hole into the next room. All the passengers called were Jewish. Many of the passengers concerned were uncomfortably reminded of events during the war – when Jews and non-Jews were separated for the most terrifying and evil of purposes. Coincidental as it was, it can't have helped that it was a German who was calling out the Jewish names.

Soon after this it was announced that a number of the hostages were to be released. General Amin claimed the credit for persuading the terrorists to make this "humanitarian gesture". The released hostages included 33 French, 2 Americans, 2 Greeks, 2 Dutch, 3 Moroccans, and 2 South Americans. All those released were non-Jews.

Another Air France plane was allowed to land at Entebbe, to take the freed hostages to Paris. The crew of the hijacked plane were told they could go with them. With incredible courage they all refused, insisting on staying with the remainder of their kidnapped passengers.

Meanwhile in Israel the authorities were considering their options. Things looked bleak. Israel's hard-line, no surrender to terrorism policy meant there was no question of giving the terrorists what they wanted – even if the other countries involved would go along.

There was little faith in the soft option of patient negotiation. The Israelis felt sure that the terrorists were almost certain to kill their hostages if their demands weren't met – or even if they were.

That left only one answer – force. A rescue operation. But the terrorists had threatened to kill all the hostages if there was any attempt at a rescue. Moreover, the hostages were held captive far away, in a hostile African country, whose ruthless ruler was known to be friendly to the terrorists.

It all seemed impossible – but it had to be done. "Operation Thunderball" was set in motion, under the command of General Dan Shomron, who would also lead the actual attack. Various plans were considered, including an invasion by boat from Kenya, across Lake Victoria. It was finally decided that an airborne attack offered the best chances of speed and surprise. Fortunately, Entebbe was in range of the Hercules transport planes which the Israelis used as troop carriers.

General Shomron began an intensive intelligence operation. By a stroke of luck an Israeli company had actually helped to build Entebbe airport, so plans of the airport and buildings were readily available. Israeli pilots who had flown into Entebbe were interrogated about conditions at the airstrip. Released hostages were contacted and questioned, and it was learned that the hostages had been moved from the plane to the terminal.

To provide time for "Operation Thunderball" to be set up, the Israelis entered into lengthy negotiations with the terrorists, arguing about arrangements for the release of the terrorist prisoners, and their exchange for the hostages. During these negotiations, over a hundred more non-Jewish hostages were released. Apart from the Air France crew who'd stayed on voluntarily, all the remaining hostages were Jews. By now the Israelis were convinced that the terrorists were determined to kill their prisoners if their demands weren't met. And there were signs that they were growing impatient. A first deadline had already passed. The terrorists were persuaded to set a second deadline – 2 p.m. on 4 July 1976.

On 3 July Israel's Prime Minister, Yitzhak Rabin, gave orders for the rescue operation to begin. That night five Hercules transports, followed by two Boeing 707s, took off from Israel. Four of the Hercules transports were to be used for the attack, the fifth was a reserve. Similarly, one Boeing was equipped as a hospital plane, the second was for back-up.

The planes flew across the Negev desert, across Saudi Arabia, over the Gulf of Suez and on over Ethiopia. In stormy weather they flew along the Kenya/Ugandan border. The Boeings headed for Nairobi in Kenya, on hand if needed. The five Hercules transports turned west over Lake Victoria, heading for Entebbe.

At 11 p.m. the first Hercules transport touched down, and opened its rear ramp. Armoured personnel carriers were unloaded and in no time at all they were speeding across the runway, filled with Israeli commandos. They were split into several different assault groups. The first began setting up beacons by the runways, in case the Ugandans cut off the power. The other groups headed for the terminal buildings. Ugandan sentries came running out, and were immediately shot down.

A terrorist appeared in the doorway, saw what was happening and ran back inside. There he and another terrorist opened fire on the hostages,

who were sprawled about the floor sleeping.
Israeli soldiers followed them inside and shot
both terrorists down – though not before several hostages had been hit. The woman hijacker
appeared, and she too was killed. Unfortunately, one terrified hostage ran for the door
– straight into Israeli machine-gun fire.

Another assault group, attacking the terrorist quarters ran into two terrorists, one of
whom threw a grenade. Both terrorists were
killed. The astonished Ugandan soldiers, too
demoralized to offer much resistance, were
soon mopped up. Within minutes of the first
plane landing, all resistance had been over-
come. The other planes were landing by now.
More commandos poured out, seizing control
of all the roads around the airport.

The dazed and astonished prisoners, including the twelve Air France crew members, were
ushered aboard an empty Hercules by Israeli
soldiers, then the plane took off, carrying them
to safety. To be on the safe side, seven MiG
fighters were blown up on the ground, making
sure there could be no Ugandan pursuit. Then,
one by one the Israeli planes took off. The
whole operation had lasted just over an hour;
106 hostages had been rescued.

The operation had cost a number of lives.
The four original hijackers had all been killed,

plus three more terrorists who had presumably joined them at Entebbe. Two hostages had been killed during the rescue; one died later in hospital. Twenty Ugandan soldiers died during the attack. The Israelis lost only two men. One was Sergeant Shurin, due to leave the army that same day. The other was the expedition's second-in-command. Lieutenant. Colonel Jonathan Netanyahu was killed by a single rifle-shot from the control tower, while supervising the assault. "Thunderball" was renamed "Operation Jonathan" in his honour.

One unfortunate hostage missed being rescued – and died later, in appalling circumstances. Mrs Dora Bloch had fallen ill and had been taken to a hospital in Entebbe. After the rescue, Ugandan troops dragged her from her hospital bed and killed her. It was the angry and humiliated General Amin's revenge: the murder of one sick and helpless old woman – the only hostage left in his power.

Despite the losses, there were huge celebrations in Israel when the freed hostages came home. Indeed, the success of the Entebbe raid was greeted with delight all over the world.

Just for once, it seemed, things had gone right, and the good guys had won. It was just like the movies – in fact they made a film about it. It was called *Raid on Entebbe*.

Iranian Embassy – London 1980

This terrorist attack, resulting from an internal struggle in Iran, was only resolved by a pitched battle in London. On the morning of 28 April 1980, five men entered the Iranian Embassy, an imposing five-storey building at Princes Gate in Knightsbridge. Suddenly they produced guns and fired shots. In a surprisingly short time, the gunmen had seized control of the entire building, taking twenty-six hostages in the process.

There were four British subjects amongst the hostages. One of them was a policeman, Trevor Lock, from the Diplomatic Patrol Group, who had been on duty at the front entrance. Although he was armed, his pistol, according to regulations, was out of sight, tucked away under his tunic. He had no chance to get at it before the men grabbed him and bundled him inside.

Two of the hostages were members of a BBC film unit, who had picked a very bad morning to apply for visas to Iran. One of them, Christopher Cramer, was wounded when the gunmen first opened fire. The second BBC man was Simeon Harris. The fourth British hostage, Ronald Morris, was a messenger working at the Embassy.

The rest of the hostages were Iranians on the Embassy staff, including a number of senior diplomats. There was also a Syrian journalist called Mustapha Karkouti.

In the initial confusion, two girls had escaped from the Embassy and given the alarm. Soon the building was surrounded by armed police, with marksmen in position on nearby roofs.

Early that afternoon, the Syrian journalist Karkouti was ordered to call the BBC World Service with the terrorists' demands. They were members of a rebel Iranian political group opposed to the Shi'ite fundamentalism of Ayatollah Khomeini.

They demanded the release of 91 Iranian political prisoners. They threatened to blow up the Embassy and kill the hostages if their demands weren't met.

The Iranian Foreign Minister said in reply that if any Embassy staff were harmed, the same number of political prisoners would be executed. He added that anyone who died for Islam went straight to heaven. He was sure that the loyal members of the Embassy staff would sooner die than see their government submit to blackmail, (Embassy staff, of course weren't able to comment). All in all, things didn't look very promising.

The siege settled down to a by-now familiar pattern. The Metropolitan Police were determined on the "softly, softly" approach that had worked so well before. Food was sent into the Embassy. The terrorists released a young woman suffering from shock, who was taken to hospital. Later, the wounded BBC man Christopher Cramer was also released. The terrorists' first deadline passed and no one was executed.

Because of its explosively political nature this siege was to present the police with some unusual problems. As the news spread, a mob of several hundred assorted protesters gathered at the Embassy. There were both pro and anti-Khomeini Iranians, supporting either the government or the terrorists. There were British and American students protesting against fundamentalist oppression, and against the holding of American hostages in Iran. The students were singing, the rival Iranians were chanting slogans at each other. There were also chanting Buddhists praying for peace.

Despite their efforts, frequent scuffles broke

out amongst the demonstrators. It didn't make the job of the police any easier.

In an effort to keep things low-key, more food and supplies of bedding were sent into the Embassy. The police started gathering intelligence about the state of affairs inside. They talked to the two girls who'd given the alarm, the woman who'd been released and the wounded BBC man. Unfortunately all three had left the Embassy right at the start of the siege, and knew little about how things stood now.

Over the weekend a number of negotiations took place. The gunmen asked to talk to Ambassadors from Algeria, Jordan and Iraq, and to the Red Cross. After talks with the police they freed another three hostages – a pregnant woman, a Pakistani man, and Mustapha Karkouti, the Iranian journalist.

By Monday the terrorists had lowered their demands, asking only for safe passage out of the country. Things seemed to be going well – until shots were heard from inside the building. In the Embassy things were suddenly starting to deteriorate. The five terrorists were holding 23 hostages, including six women. They were held on the second floor at the back, men in one room, women in the other. In the Arab tradition, the women expressed fear and grief by constant screaming and wailing. It didn't help anyone's nerves.

Amongst the male captives was PC Lock, still with his gun hidden under his tunic, desperately trying to keep it hidden from his captors. Constantly under armed guard he had no chance to use the gun. He was convinced that his captors would kill him if they discovered he was armed.

By now the gunmen were becoming angry and confused. They were receiving reassuring messages from the police – and angry death threats from the Iranian government and its fanatical Khomeini supporters. They were growing increasingly paranoid as the siege wore on, and suddenly refused to accept any more food. In the most sinister development of all, one of the male hostages, a young Iranian diplomat, was selected from the group and taken away.

Just before 7 p.m. on Monday evening, the terrorists opened the front door of the Embassy – and threw out the body of the young Iranian diplomat.

He had been shot dead – executed in cold blood. The terrorists sent a message. The next execution would follow in less than an hour. Unless the police agreed to their demands, more hostages would be killed.

The police hastened to agree with all the terrorists' demands. Urging them to stay calm, they said details of their safe conduct were being arranged. The real plan was very different.

Some time earlier, realizing that a peaceful end to the siege was now unlikely, the authorities had called in the Special Air Service (SAS), who had prepared an assault plan.

Soon after 7 p.m., the Home Secretary gave the order to go ahead. Suddenly black-clad men in balaclavas appeared on the Embassy balcony. Blowing in the windows and hurling smoke-grenades they vanished into the building. At the rear of the building, more black-clad figures abseiled down from the roof, blowing in windows and swinging inside. Smoke and flame billowed from the Embassy windows, shots were heard – and the first freed hostages began stumbling on to the balcony. One of them was the other BBC man, Simeon Harris.

Inside the Embassy, the sudden attack took the terrorists by surprise. As the first SAS man entered, the terrorist leader raised his gun to shoot him. PC Lock grappled with him and after a brief struggle the SAS man shot the terrorist dead.

The other terrorists opened fire on the

hostages, killing one and seriously wounding three others. The SAS men shot them down. When the brief battle was over, all but one of the terrorists was dead. Policemen, firemen and ambulance men moved into the building. Meanwhile the black-clad soldiers of the SAS quietly faded away. It was their first "public" appearance – the beginning of the SAS legend.

The Iranian Embassy siege provides some useful lessons about the hard approach to terrorism. If force is to be used, it must be unexpected, swift, and devastatingly effective.

Dithering between the hard and soft approach, half-hearted attacks followed by force used too late – all this can only lead to disaster. Events at Waco, Texas, provide a terrible example.

Waco – 1993

Koresh and the Branch Davidians

David Koresh was an example of a particularly American phenomenon – the charismatic religious leader with hordes of fanatical followers. Koresh was born in 1959, the illegitimate child of a fifteen-year-old mother. Brought up by a fanatically religious grandmother, he showed early signs of religious mania, studying the Bible obsessively and spending long hours weeping and praying.

After a disturbed and violent childhood, and a failed career as a rock star, he joined a minor religious sect called the Branch Davidians, and soon rose to become its leader. Koresh had an encyclopaedic knowledge of the Scriptures and a dominating, and charismatic personality. Most of his deluded followers genuinely believed he was the returned Christ, the Son of God. Somehow this belief survived his habit of having sex with his female disciples, often with girls as young as thirteen. Many children were born into the cult, most of them his.

Under Koresh's leadership the Davidians became a successful and prosperous cult. They drew members from many countries, including Great Britain. The base of the cult was Mount Carmel, a 77-acre ranch in Waco, Texas, 90 miles north of Dallas. Over a hundred people lived there, men, women and children. About a third were British.

Koresh and his followers combined religious fanaticism with another treasured American tradition – the right to bear arms. The sect had a paranoid fear and hatred of the outside world. Mount Carmel became a fortified compound, holding a vast stockpile of weapons. A network of bunkers and tunnels was constructed beneath the ranch. Koresh laid in supplies of food and water. It was as if he knew a clash with the authorities was inevitable – as if he welcomed it.

The clash, when it came, was with the Bureau of Alcohol Tobacco and Firearms – the ATA. This is a relatively obscure federal agency, concerned with offences in these areas. (Their most – indeed their only – famous member was Elliot Ness, who battled bootleggers in thirties Chicago.)

Concerned with allegations of illegal arms and child abuse within the compound, 200 agents of the ATA staged a secret raid on Mount Carmel on 28 February 1993. But somehow the secret had leaked out – Koresh and his followers were ready and waiting. In a brief and bloody shootout, the Davidians defended themselves with automatic weapons – and a howitzer! Four ATA agents were killed, and sixteen wounded. A handful of cult members were killed, including, Koresh claimed, his own son, before the defeated ATA agents retired.

The death of the four agents put Koresh and his followers high on the wanted list. The ranch was surrounded by 500 federal agents – and the siege dragged on for an incredible 51 days.

The publicity-loving Koresh kept the authorities dangling, making frequent phone calls, several radio broadcasts, and even negotiating a book contract. He said he was awaiting instructions from God about his surrender. He was, however, persuaded to let some of his followers leave. 21 children left the ranch – but there were 25 more still inside. The Davidians had ample supplies of food and water – there was a well inside the compound – and plenty of arms and ammunition. They were prepared for a long siege.

It was decided that the ATA were too inexperienced to cope with the situation, and the FBI took over. At dawn on 19 April they contacted the compound and issued an ultimatum. Unless the Davidians surrendered immediately, the FBI would attack. Forewarned of the FBI's intentions, the Davidians were defiant, throwing the telephone out of the window. The FBI moved in.

By now the Army was involved as well. A *tank* smashed down the door of the main building, and lobbed canisters of CS gas inside.

Later, another tank blew a hole in the side of the building and more gas shells were fired inside. Confidently, the FBI waited for the Davidians to surrender. Nothing happened. It's believed that they probably took shelter in the tunnels beneath the building, where the gas didn't penetrate. Pausing only to hold a couple of press conferences, the FBI made another gas attack.

Suddenly smoke was seen billowing from the buildings. Two of the cult members, later captured, had set fire to the ranch. Soon the entire building was ablaze. High winds fanned the blaze and soon hidden ammunition dumps started to explode. With horrifying speed the entire compound was destroyed in a roaring inferno. David Koresh and everyone inside the building – including 21 children – died in the flames.

Largely because of the children's deaths, the FBI came in for massive criticism after the siege was over. For one thing, nobody had thought to have the Fire Brigade standing by. It took hours for them to reach the scene, by which time it was too late.

The two captured cult members denied setting fire to the building. They claimed that the tanks had started the blaze, knocking over oil lamps. The FBI insisted that the Davidians had started the fires themselves. Forensic evidence later showed that children and other cult members had been executed, killed by their fellow Davidians before the flames took hold.

Criticism of the way the siege had been handled went all the way up to the newly-elected President Clinton. There can be no doubt that the FBI made mistakes, but they had an incredibly difficult task. They were trying to save the lives of a group of religious fanatics who didn't fear death. Fanatics led by a man who seemed to welcome his own fiery martyrdom.

HORRIBLE CRIMES

Crime is another argument for the theory put forward in the previous chapter – the most dangerous beast on the planet is man. We can follow the twisted logic of the terrorist – the end justifies the means – even if we can't agree with it. But with the criminals in this chapter, we're dealing with the mystery of evil – with human monsters and motives beyond our understanding. One of the worst was a medieval monster called Gilles de Rais.

Gilles de Rais

One thing you couldn't possibly say about Gilles de Rais was that he came from a deprived background. He was born in 1420, into one of the noblest families in Brittany. His father died when Gilles was 20, and the young man became rich and powerful. He owned an enormous estate and he was related to all the most powerful families in France.

He was a tall, handsome young man, with hair and beard so black that they looked almost blue. Courteous and scholarly, in his youth Gilles seemed the ideal young aristocrat. He served King Charles VI of France in the wars against the English, and fought under Joan of Arc in the Siege of Orleans. The grateful king rewarded him with the rank of Marshal of France.

Gilles retired to his Castle of Champtoce, where he lived in the most sumptuous style imaginable. He was surrounded by hundreds of richly dressed retainers, gave lavish banquets for the neighbouring nobility, held splendid tournaments, and gave generously to the poor. At the same time he was very religious, keeping a large staff of priests and his own choir.

Deciding it was time he took a wife, Gilles married Catherine de Thouars, a noble heiress, in a magnificent ceremony. Every thing looked set fair for the wealthy young nobleman – but things were just beginning to go wrong. Gilles was living in such an extravagant style that even his huge estates couldn't stand the strain. He was starting to run short of money. He was still a rich man and could easily have managed by economizing, but Gilles was too vain to do that. He had been too wealthy for too long, and couldn't face the shame of being seen to cut down.

He turned instead to one of the most dangerous illusions of the Middle Ages – the quest for the Philosophers' Stone. This, as everyone knew, enabled you to change common metal into gold. Once he had found it all his troubles would be over. He sent messengers all over France, and to Italy, Spain and Germany as well, asking for alchemists to help him. Hordes of them turned up and Gilles built a magnificent and extremely expensive laboratory in one of the towers in his castle. For a whole year furnaces blazed and alchemists carried out strange and costly experiments – living meanwhile in the utmost luxury at Gilles' expense.

The alchemists would have been happy to go on for ever, but Gilles was getting impatient. He was spending more money than ever and had nothing to show for it.

One of the alchemists, an Italian called Prelati, told Gilles of a possible short cut. If he would dedicate himself to the service of Satan, the answer could be found more quickly. Gilles agreed. The other alchemists were dismissed, the entrance to the tower was sealed and no one was allowed to enter. Catherine, Gilles' wife, who was pregnant by now, found that her husband became increasingly strange and distant. He spent long hours in the sealed tower, where mysterious lights burned through the night.

Sinister rumours began circulating around the countryside – rumours about missing children. Prelati, the Italian alchemist, became alarmed and vanished from the castle.

Gilles told his wife he was going on a pilgrimage to the Holy Land. Warning her to stay away from the sealed tower he set off. Catherine's sister Anne came to stay with her to keep her company while Gilles was away.

Left alone with her sister, Catherine found the mystery of the sealed tower preying on her mind. She told Anne about Gilles' strange behaviour, about the lights in the tower – and about the missing children. . .

Curiosity overcoming their fears, the sisters determined to investigate the tower. Since the door was sealed, they decided that there must be a concealed entrance. Searching the room nearest to the tower they found a copper stud concealed behind a sculpture. They pressed it and a secret door slid open, revealing a flight of stone stairs.

The two young women climbed the steps into the dark and gloomy tower. On the first floor they found a chapel, where oil lamps were still burning. The cross on the wall was upside down and the candles on the altar were black. It was a Satanist chapel.

On the second floor was a room filled with alembics, crucibles and furnaces – all the apparatus of an alchemist's laboratory .

On the third floor they found a darkened room, which gave off a terrible rotting stench . . .

They went on into the darkened room, and Catherine stumbled into some kind of vessel which she knocked over. Her feet and the bottom of her dress became soaked with some thick fluid. Retreating to the staircase, she realized that she was covered in blood.

Anne wanted to leave, but Catherine was determined to discover the truth. She went back to the chapel, picked up a lamp and returned to the dark room. There she saw a sight of the utmost horror. All around the room were copper vessels, filled to the brim with blood. Each vessel bore a date. On a black marble table in the centre of the room lay the body of a newly-murdered child.

Terrified that her husband would learn that she had discovered his secret, Catherine desperately tried to clean up the spilled blood. But despite all her efforts, the stain only seemed to spread more and more.

Suddenly she heard the clatter of horses in the courtyard outside, and the shouts of the servants, "My lord has returned!" Panicking, Anne fled upwards to the battlements.

Catherine ran down the stairs. Outside the Satanist chapel she found herself facing her husband, and the evil alchemist Prelati. They dragged her inside.

Prelati looked at Catherine and said, "As you see, the victim has come of her own accord."

"Begin the Black Mass," said Gilles. He went to a cupboard, took out a sacrificial knife, and

The Alchemist's Laboratory

went to stand over his wife, who had collapsed on a bench, swooning with fear.

Instead of going to the Holy Land, Gilles had gone after Prelati, who was living in Nantes. Tracking him down, he had threatened the alchemist with death unless he made good his promise to deliver the Philosophers' Stone. Playing for time, Prelati told him that Satan demanded one final sacrifice – the lives of Catherine and her unborn child. Gilles immediately set off for his castle, forcing Prelati to accompany him.

While the terrible ceremony went on, Catherine's sister Anne was up on the battlements of the tower, scanning the surrounding countryside for help. To her relief she saw a party of mounted men approaching the castle. As they came closer she recognised her two brothers, who had come to visit Catherine while her husband was away. Frantically, Anne waved her veil.

As the Black Mass reached its climax, Gilles heard the party riding into the castle courtyard, and the servants announcing the arrival of Catherine's brothers.

Turning to his terrified wife he said, "Madame, I forgive you. The matter is at an end between us if you now do as I tell you."

Catherine was to change out of her blood-soaked dress and join her husband in greeting her brothers. She was to behave normally and give them no cause for suspicion. If she did, she would be brought back to the chapel after their departure and the interrupted Black Mass would be concluded – ending in her death.

Soon afterwards, Gilles was receiving his visitors in the main hall of the castle. Then Catherine came to join them, her face a ghastly white. Gilles fixed her with a hypnotic stare.

One of her brothers asked if she was ill. Catherine said it was nothing, simply her pregnancy. Then, as Gilles talked to the other brother, she whispered, "Save me, he seeks to kill me."

Suddenly her sister Anne ran into the room. "Take us away," she cried. "This man is an assassin!" She pointed to Gilles. The brothers and their escort drew their swords, surrounding the two sisters. Gilles called for his men-at-arms, but his servants refused to fight. The brothers got their sisters safely across the drawbridge and out of the castle.

Catherine's terrible story added to the rumours that had been spreading throughout the countryside. It wasn't easy to move against a Marshal of France, but eventually the scandal grew so great that the Church was forced to act. The Bishop of Nantes petitioned the Duke of Brittany, who sent men to arrest Gilles and his accomplice Prelati. Searching the tower, the Duke's men uncovered the dreadful evidence of Gilles' crimes – the rotting remains of scores of dead children.

Gilles was brought to trial before the Duke of Brittany, the Bishop of Nantes, the Vicar of the Inquisition and the President of the Provincial Parliament, accused of murder and sorcery.

At first Gilles maintained a scornful attitude, saying that he would sooner be hanged without trial than plead before such knaves. But Prelati had made a full confession, and as the terrible revelations horrified the court, Gilles broke down and confessed.

Nearly a hundred children had been sacrificed to Satan in his frenzied quest for the Philosophers' Stone. Gilles and Prelati were both found guilty and sentenced to be burned alive. However, in view of Gilles' high rank, his sentence was reduced. He was to be strangled first. The sentence was carried out at Nantes, on 23 February 1440.

According to a chronicler of the time, Gilles de Rais "made a very devout end, full of penitence, most humbly imploring his Creator to have mercy on his manifold sins and wickedness."

The remains of the Castle of Champtoce still stand. It is said that on dark nights Gilles' hideous half-burned body can be seen on the ruined battlements, glowing with all the fires of hell. Inside the ruined walls wail the ghosts of his innocent victims.

As time went by, the story of Gilles de Rais, much altered and embellished, passed into folk-tales and legends. Oddly enough, one detail of the true story survived. It concerns his beard, so black that it looked almost blue. In the legends, Gilles de Rais is known as Bluebeard.

The English are said have a traditional love of a good gruesome murder – and the most gruesome series of murders of all was committed in Victorian times.

The killer is still undetected but after more than a hundred years, his name still strikes terror. It conjures up pictures of lonely footsteps hurrying through the swirling fog of cobbled alleyways. A cloaked figure follows swiftly, with a gleaming knife hidden under the cloak. . .

His real name is still unknown, but he calls himself Jack – Jack the Ripper. . .

Jack the Ripper – 1888

The year, of course, is the year of Jack the Ripper's crimes. The year of his birth, like the year of his death, is unknown – though there are plenty of theories. The facts, as far as they are known, are these . . .

All the Ripper murders took place in London's East End, a lively, brawling place filled with cheap shops, doss houses, gin palaces, and brothels. The huge, bustling market that straggled along Petticoat Lane was said to be crammed with stolen goods. Today its somewhat more respectable successor is still a big tourist attraction. The East End of the 1880s was a place of great poverty and a centre of petty crime. Close to the docks, its lively pubs were an attraction for paid-off sailors with money to spend.

In those pre-welfare days, the very poor were often driven to crime simply to survive. For men it was usually robbery. For women it was prostitution. Most of the Ripper's wretched victims were women on the edge of destitution, desperately trying to earn the price of a drink, a meal, or a bed for the night.

Even the date of the Ripper's first murder isn't absolutely certain. The East End was a violent place at the best of times, and knife-attacks on women were not unknown. However, it seems likely that the first Ripper murder took place in Whitechapel on the night of 6 August 1888, a bank holiday.

Next morning a waterside labourer called Reeves left his lodging in George Yard Buildings at dawn on his way to work. On the first floor landing he found the huddled body of a woman lying in a pool of blood. Horrified, he ran out into the street, returning a few minutes later with a policeman.

The policeman sent for a doctor, who had the body taken to the local morgue. It was found to be that of a plump, middle-aged woman. She had been stabbed – about forty times.

This first crime didn't cause much of a stir,

although the *Star* newspaper headlined it as:

A WHITECHAPEL HORROR

No one in George Buildings knew who the woman was, but eventually a warehouseman called Tabram came forward, and identified her as his wife. They had been separated for years, and Martha Tabram, who had a drink problem, had turned to prostitution.

She had been seen with two soldiers earlier – and that same night a constable on the beat had seen a soldier hanging about. The police made enquiries at the Grenadier Guards barracks in the nearby Tower of London, but they came to nothing.

Like Martha Tabram, the next victim, Polly Nichols was a prostitute. By now Polly was on the bottom rung of the business. She was middle-aged, penniless and very often drunk. On the night of 30 August 1888, she turned up at her usual doss-house, tipsy as usual. She was turned away because she didn't have the fourpence it cost for a bed – she'd spent all her money on a new bonnet.

Undaunted, Polly asked the doss house woman to save her a bed while she went out and found a new customer. "I'll soon get my doss money," she said. "See what a jolly bonnet I've got now!"

Outside the doss house, Polly ran into an old friend called Ellen Holland, who offered her a bed. Polly refused, and staggered off along the Whitechapel Road. It was the last time Ellen saw her alive.

At 3.45 a.m. on 31 August, a patrolling policeman found Polly Nichols lying dead on the pavement in Bucks Row, Whitechapel. Her body was lying across the entrance to a stable yard. Her throat had been cut, so savagely that the head was almost severed. A post-mortem revealed extensive mutilations to the body. When news of the crime spread, Ellen Holland came forward and identified the body of her friend.

Once again, police enquiries produced no results. The constable who found the body had passed that way half an hour earlier. There had been no body then. Three men working nearby in a slaughterhouse, and a nightwatchman guarding the sewage works, had seen and heard nothing. Polly had been strangled before her throat was cut, which may explain why nobody heard any screams.

Some claim that Polly Nichols was the Ripper's *first* victim. (Martha Tabram had been savagely stabbed, but not mutilated.) In any event, the second bloody murder so soon after the first caused a great public outcry. In true tabloid style the *Star* headline screamed:

A REVOLTING MURDER
Ghastly Crimes By A Maniac

The *Star* also published a lurid account of a mysterious character called "Leather Apron", a leather worker who prowled the East End, extorting money from prostitutes by threatening them with a knife. Surprisingly enough, this character really did exist. He was man called John Pizer, undoubtedly a nasty piece of work. But when he was later found by the police he had alibis for the times of the murders and they had to release him.

Drawn by morbid curiosity, crowds of sight-seers gathered in Buck's Row, examining the spot where the body had been found. Nothing happened for the next few days, but the atmosphere in the East End remained tense. Everyone was waiting for the murderer to strike again.

On Saturday 8 September, the body of a woman was found in the back yard of a house in Hanbury Street. The body had been more horribly mutilated than Polly's.

The victim, a woman in her late forties, was a prostitute called Annie Chapman, known as Dark Annie. On the evening before her death, Annie had been sitting in the kitchen of her lodging house in Dorset Street. Like Polly Nichols, Annie was fond of a drink, and she'd spent her lodging money. Like Polly, she asked the lodging house keeper to save her a bed, and went out into the dark streets to earn the money for it. And, like Polly, she met Jack the Ripper.

Although Annie's body had been found in the yard of a crowded boarding house, once again no one had seen or heard anything. Like Polly, she had been strangled before having her throat cut. The body had been extensively mutilated. Some of the internal organs had been placed beside the body. Others had been removed altogether. The doctor concerned reported that the removal of the organs had been carried out with a certain amount of surgical skill. This gave rise to one of the Ripper legends, that the murderer was a distinguished surgeon who had gone insane.

Another, even more grisly theory was that the murder had been committed just to obtain the missing organs. Tales circulated of a mysterious American who had been offering vast sums for fresh human organs in good condition.

This third and bloodiest murder sent the East End into a panic. The newspapers were full of nothing else, and newsagents sold out for miles around. The *Star* insisted that "The ghoul-like creature who stalks through the streets of London, hunting down his victim. . . is drunk with blood. He will have more ."

Angry mobs gathered in Buck's Row and in Hanbury Street, and surrounded police stations and mortuaries. More respectable folk showed their concerns as well. Local business men formed the Mile End Vigilance Committee and offered a reward of £100, a great sum in those days.

By now the Ripper case was in the hands of Inspector Abberline, one of the Metropolitan Police's most experienced detectives. But

Abberline was getting nowhere. Several suspects were arrested and questioned and later
released. One of the most promising was a
mad Russian butcher who was in the habit of
carrying butcher knives about with him, and
threatening to rip people up. But although he
was undoubtedly mad, there was no evidence
connecting him with the crimes.

As time went on and there were no more murders, the panic faded, and life in the East End returned to something like normal. Pubs and cafés became busy again, and even the prostitutes went back to plying their dangerous trade. They had no alternative – it was that or starve. Then came the most horrifying event of all. On the night of 30 September there were two murders in one night.

The first body was found at 1 a.m. in the yard of the International Working Men's Educational Club in Dutton Street. There had been a Saturday night debate and several members were still inside, talking and singing. The club steward was a part-time pedlar as well. He was coming back to the club with his horse and cart, to store his unsold stock, when he saw a huddled form in the yard and realized it was the body of a woman. The steward rushed into the club and told the members there was a woman in the yard. He didn't know whether she was drunk or dead.

Morris Eagle, the chairman of the club, went out to investigate. He saw blood flowing from a terrible gash in the woman's throat and forming a pool around the body, and ran into the street to call the police.

Morris Eagle was in luck. Almost immediately he ran into a patrolling constable in the street and brought him back. The constable examined the body.

It was still warm . . .

Mitre Square lies off Aldgate, just three-quarters of a mile from Dutton Street. At 1.45 a.m. a patrolling constable entered the square. In a dimly-lit corner he saw the most horrible sight of his career. It was the dead body of a woman, her throat cut and her stomach ripped open. Her face had been mutilated as well.

The constable had checked Mitre Square just a quarter of an hour before. Inside just fifteen minutes, the Ripper had lured his second victim into the dark square, butchered her and vanished into the night. As usual, no one had seen or heard anything. Once again, some of the internal organs were found to be missing.

There was a gruesome sequel. The police searched the area around the square for clues – and one of them found a strange message. Written in white chalk on the black bricks edging a doorway were the words:

"The Juwes are the men That Will not be Blamed for Nothing."

Beneath the message lay a piece of blood-soaked apron, torn from the dead woman's clothing – as if to confirm that the message really did come from the murderer himself.

The message was carefully copied and photographed. Then, by the orders of Sir Charles Warren, the Police Commissioner, the message was wiped away with a wet sponge. He feared that if the message was left on display, so close to the scene of two savage murders, it might provoke anti-Jewish riots. The message, with its strange misspelling "Juwes" has never been explained. Even the meaning is obscure. Possibly it was a clumsy attempt by the murderer to put the blame for his crimes on the local Jewish community. Sir Charles was much criticized later for wiping out what might have been a

vital clue, but he always insisted that he had done the right thing.

Now the police had two unidentified bodies on their hands. But that part of the mystery at least was soon solved.

The woman in Dutton Street turned out to be a charwoman and occasional prostitute known as Long Liz. Swedish in origin, she had lived in England for many years, and had taken the name of Elizabeth Stride.

The Mitre Square victim was called Kate Kelly, described as "a right jolly sort". She was living with a man called John Kelly, a market labourer, and had taken his name. On the last day of her life Kate was arrested for being drunk. After sleeping it off in a cell she was released late that night. The police station was only a few minutes' walk away from Mitre Square. Soon after Kate Kelly went out into the night she must have met a cloaked figure – who took her into Mitre Yard and killed her.

The double murder provoked more uproar than ever before, and the police were heavily criticized. To be fair, they had a difficult task. Their usual methods simply didn't work. Most murders were committed for gain, or were crimes of passion. But there was no link between this killer and his victims, no motive except what the papers called "the thirst for blood".

The police were flooded with false leads, and with reports from people who claimed to have seen the murdered women with sinister, foreign-looking men just before their deaths. None of this information turned out to be of the slightest use. Then came the first letter. Long, rambling and boastful, written in red ink, it was sent to the Central News Agency. The letter began: "Dear Boss, I keep on hearing that the police have caught me but they wont fix me just yet. I have laughed when they look so clever and talk about being on the right track. That joke about Leather Apron gave me real fits." The writer went on to say that he was "down on whores" and wouldn't stop killing until he was caught. He threatened to send the next victim's ears to the police "just for jolly". The letter ended: "My knife's so nice and sharp I want to get to work right away if I get a chance." It was signed, "Yours truly, Jack the Ripper."

It was only after this letter that the name "Jack the Ripper" came into common use. Before the letter, the murderer was usually called Leather Apron, after the suspect the police had released.

The police took the letter seriously enough to make facsimiles of it and distribute them around the East End. The only result was to provoke a flood of other "Ripper" letters, most of them obvious fakes, though they all had to be investigated.

One, however, bore chilling evidence of being genuine.

The chairman of the Mile End Vigilance Committee, the organization offering a reward for the Ripper's capture, received a small parcel in the mail. When opened it contained half a human kidney, and a misspelled note headed: "From hell".

The note went on: "I send you half the kidne I took from one women presarved it for you tother piece I fried and ate it was very nise I may send you the bloody knife that took it out if you only wate a whil longer. Catch me if you can."

The horrified chairman sent the parcel to a pathologist, who gave his opinion that it was a human kidney, probably female, and had been taken from a heavy drinker . . .

Once again fear returned to the East End. There were few people about at night. The narrow streets became more terrifying than ever when October brought thick fogs. The police mounted a massive house-to-house search of all Whitechapel. It was feared this might cause trouble, but nobody complained – everyone wanted the Ripper caught.

The search produced nothing.

More than a month went by and there had been no more murders. As autumn turned to winter, the streetwalkers returned to their trade . . .

Mary Kelly was a cut above the rest of the Ripper's victims. She was young and attractive with long fair hair. She was a bit better off as well. She actually had a room of her own, at 13 Millers Court, just off Dorset Street.

She was, however, behind with her rent. On the morning of Friday 9 November, Lord Mayor's Day, her landlord, a local shopkeeper, sent his young assistant round to try and collect.

The assistant knocked on the door but got no answer. One of the windows was broken, so he reached in and pulled the curtain aside. What he saw sent him running back to his boss.

"I knocked on the door and could not make anyone answer," he said. "I looked in the window and saw a lot of blood . . ." The landlord followed him back to Millers Court and looked in through the window. He saw Mary Kelly's butchered body lying on the bed. There was blood all over the room. The landlord sent his assistant running to the local police station, and very soon the police were on the scene, followed by the police surgeon. Mary's remains were taken to the morgue and the police began their investigation.

Once again it produced nothing. The killer had left no clues to his identity. The murder followed the same pattern as the others, except that the mutilations were even more extensive. The privacy of Mary's room had given the murderer time to carry out his savage butchery uninterrupted. Once again witnesses came forward claiming to have seen Mary with various sinister-looking men on the night before her death. Many suspects were brought in and questioned. Once again, the police enquiries led nowhere.

The latest murder aroused the usual panic, the usual outrage, and the usual criticisms of the police, but there is something very special about this murder. It was the last that can be definitely attributed to Jack the Ripper. As time went on and there were no more Ripper killings, the extra police patrols were brought to an end, and the panic died down. Only the terrible memory of Jack the Ripper remained – a memory that haunts us to this day.

There are several reasons why Jack the Ripper became a legend. There is something baffling about the way the string of killings suddenly came to an end. The fact that Jack was never caught has given rise to endless theorizing about his true identity.

These last two questions are often linked. Although it's possible that the Ripper's blood-lust was sated by the final killing, it's very unlike serial killers suddenly just to stop. Could it be that Jack stopped killing for other reasons – because he himself was dead, for instance?

Who was the Ripper? One candidate for the Jack the Ripper role is a barrister called Montague John Druitt, who suffered a mental breakdown, and committed suicide. His dead body was found in the river in December 1888, just over a month after the last murder. He is said to have been under suspicion, by his own relatives and by the police. However, no actual evidence links him to the crimes. Other police suspects at the time included a Pole called Kosminski, and a Russian called Ostrog. Both were dangerously insane and both were eventually confined in asylums. Once again, there is a complete lack of any real evidence.

Theories about the true identity of Jack the Ripper are still being produced today. One of the more fanciful is that the Ripper was really a dissolute young member of the Royal Family. Prince Albert Victor, Duke of Clarence, led a rackety life which caused his family much concern. He died of pneumonia in 1892. This theory asserts that the killer was never caught because of a massive cover-up involving "the highest in the land".

Almost every year seems to produce a new Jack the Ripper book, with a new solution to the mystery of his identity. A new and even more amazing theory recently emerged with the appearance of a document alleged to be Jack the Ripper's Diary. According to this, the Ripper was a man called James Maybrick, a wealthy Liverpool cotton merchant. The diary reveals that Maybrick knew that his wife was being unfaithful to him. Insane with jealousy, he made regular trips to London and relieved his angry feelings by murdering prostitutes in the East End.

James Maybrick died in 1889, a year after the last murder. His wife Florence was later accused of poisoning him with arsenic from flypapers. So, Jack the Ripper stopped murdering because he was murdered! A neat theory with the advantage of combining two famous crimes.

Jack the Ripper theories seem to grow wilder as time goes on, and we shall probably never know the Ripper's real identity. In his ghastly way he was something of a pioneer. He was probably the first recorded example of the serial killer – the murderer who has no connection with his victims and kills for the pleasure of it.

Whoever the Ripper was he must of course be dead by now. But today, when serial killers are commonplace, crimes all over the world prove that "Yours truly, Jack the Ripper" is very much with us in spirit . . .

The Holocaust and Anne Frank

We come now to the greatest crime of the twentieth century – in fact, to the greatest crime of all time. The Holocaust is the term commonly used to describe an indescribable horror – the murder of around six million Jews by the Nazis in the

Second World War. The truly horrific thing about
the Holocaust is that it was a crime organized by
a government. It wasn't easy killing six million
people – it required a lot of hard work, a lot of
organization, and the support of a specially
created bureaucracy.

Nazi policy had always been a grab-bag of
popular ideas, and it was never short of scape-
goats. Communists, capitalists, intellectuals,
trade unionists, gays, gypsies and above all
Jews – you name it and the Nazis were
against it. However, the Nazis did not invent
anti-Semitism; it had always been present in
Germany and Austria, and Hitler simply
included it in official Nazi policy.

The persecution began in 1933, when the
Nazis came to power in Germany. Jews were
banned from the civil service and Jewish doctors were forbidden to work in hospitals. Jews
were excluded from cultural and business
activities. Nazi thugs beat up Jews in the
streets. The police were forbidden to interfere
on the Jew's behalf. More anti-Jewish laws
were announced at the Nuremberg Rally in
1935. In 1938 the assassination of a German
diplomat in Paris by a Polish Jew sparked off
a systematic attack on Jewish property all
over Germany. So many windows were broken
that the event was called *Kristallnacht*, the

Night of the (Broken) Glass. All this was quite bad enough – but far more terrible plans were being made.

There was no room in Germany's prisons for everyone Hitler wanted to lock up, so special concentration camps were built where thousands of captives were sent. The commandant of one of the camps, at Auschwitz, received orders to begin killing Jews in May 1941. Plans for a "final solution" of what the Nazis called the "Jewish Problem" were finalized at the Wannsee Conference in January 1942. Adolf Eichmann was given responsibility for the complicated details.

The extermination system centred on Nazi-occupied Poland. More death camps were set up at Maidanek, Treblinka, Chelmno, and Sobibor. Auschwitz, the first, was one of the most notorious. At its busiest it held 100 000 prisoners at a time, and gassed 12 000 of a them a *day*, burning the bodies in special ovens.

The prisoners arrived by train, crammed into cattle-trucks, without food or water. SS doctors met the trains as they arrived .

The passengers, men, women and children, were briefly examined as they arrived. The strongest were sent into the camp to be worked to death, the others were told they

were going to the showers. In fact they were sent straight to the gas chambers.

At the war crimes tribunal at Nuremberg after the war, the commandant of Auschwitz described how a gas called Zyclon B, made from crystallized prussic acid, was used: "It took from three to fifteen minutes to kill all the people in the death-chamber, depending on climatic conditions. We knew when the people were dead because the screaming stopped. We usually waited for half an hour before we opened the doors and removed the bodies. After the bodies were removed, a squad of prisoners took off the rings and extracted the gold teeth of the corpses."

Rumours of what was happening to the Jews had been leaking out of Nazi-occupied Europe for years, but it wasn't until 1945 that the full horror was revealed. The advancing Allies overran the camps, and the world was shocked by newsreel film of piles of unburned bodies left behind by the fleeing Nazis, and of the walking skeletons that were the few starving survivors.

Anne Frank

The Holocaust is a crime of such vast proportions that it's almost impossible to understand — six million deaths are just too many for the mind to take in.

The tragic story of Anne Frank and her family helps to bring the Holocaust into focus.

Otto Frank, Anne's father, was born in Frankfurt, Germany, into a prosperous Jewish middle-class banking family. He had been an officer in the German army in the First World War. Because times were so hard in Germany after the war, Otto Frank moved to Amsterdam, and went into business there, first in banking, and later in the herb and spice business.

By 1939, Otto Frank, his wife Edith and his two daughters, Margot and Anne, were established in Amsterdam, with a prosperous business and a comfortable apartment. Otto Frank knew of the danger from the Nazis, but he believed that the Germans would respect Dutch neutrality. Sadly, he was wrong. The Nazis invaded and occupied Holland in 1940, and soon began introducing anti-Jewish laws. Otto Frank had to resign from the board of his business and hand over control to "Aryan", i.e. non-Jewish, directors. Anne, a cheerful friendly girl of twelve, and her fifteen-year-old sister Margot had to leave their school and their many non-Jewish friends and attend a special school, where all the pupils and teachers were Jewish. Jews were forbidden to use buses, or the swimming pool, or to go out at night. If they went out in the daytime they had to wear a big yellow star on the back of their coats.

All these petty restrictions were bad enough, but there was worse to come. In 1941 the Germans began rounding up Amsterdam's Jews. They were sent first to transit camps, then onward to the death camps. No one ever came back.

Otto Frank decided on a desperate plan. His herb and spice business was situated in an office block on the Prinsengracht canal. The building had a disused area that had once been a warehouse. Otto set up simple living quarters for himself and his family in this "secret annexe". The annexe was entered by a secret door hidden behind a bookcase.

One night the Frank family left their comfortable apartment and vanished into the annexe. There they were joined by another family, a Mrs and Mrs Van Daan, their son Peter, a boy of about Anne's age, and by Mr Dussel, an elderly dentist.

Incredibly, they remained in hiding for over two years. Otto Frank's loyal employees kept them supplied with food.

Just before the Frank family went into hiding, Anne started a diary. It tells of her life in confinement. Anne paints a vivid picture of the strains and stresses of a group of people shut up together in a small space. The fugitives were in constant danger, unable ever to go outside.

In this strange and restricted setting Anne struggled with the problems of growing up, and of family relationships. Inevitably, she and Peter Van Daan fell in love. Anne emerges from the pages of this diary as a lively, sensitive, highly intelligent young girl, eager for life. Although she didn't know it at the time, not much more life was left for her.

The tragedy is that Anne Frank and her family and friends so nearly made it. By 1944 the Germans were on the run. D-Day and the liberation of Europe were not far away. Then, in August 1944, Gestapo agents entered the building, went straight to the secret door, and arrested all those in hiding. The Franks had been betrayed.

During the arrest, one of the Gestapo men picked up a briefcase to look for valuables. He found it held nothing but papers and threw them on the floor. Amongst the papers was Anne's diary.

After their arrest, the fugitives were sent to the transit camp at Westerbork, where they spent the whole of August. A witness reports that Anne and Peter were always together, and that Anne looked radiantly happy. It was to be the last happiness of her short life. At the beginning of September, they were all sent on to Auschwitz. There the men were separated from the women. Mr Van Daan and old Mr Dussel both went to the gas chambers. The women were taken to the women's block, where Mrs Frank died, along with hundreds of others in the terrible conditions. Mrs Van Daan and her son Peter were taken from the camp.

Both died on one of the "death marches" between one camp and another.

After a few months, Anne and Margot were transferred to the concentration camp at Bergen-Belsen. Ironically this was one of the "better" camps. No killings were carried out there, and there was little ill-treatment. But conditions were terrible. It was November by now, cold and wet, and women were crowded into tents with only straw to sleep on. Sanitation was primitive, food short and medicine non-existent. Administration in the camp was breaking down as the defeat of the Nazis approached.

In March 1945 a typhoid epidemic swept the camp, killing hundreds. Margot was one of the early victims. Anne Frank herself died a few days later.

Of all those who had hidden in the "secret annexe" Otto Frank, Anne's father, was the only one to survive. He stayed on in Auschwitz, and was liberated by the Russians in January 1945. After the war he returned to Amsterdam and made his way back to the annexe. Anne's diaries were still lying in the corner where the Gestapo agent had thrown them. "If he had taken the diary with him," said Otto Frank later, "no one would ever have heard of my daughter."

Soon after the war, Otto Frank arranged to have Anne's diary published. It made a tremendous sensation, touching the conscience of the world. It was translated into over thirty languages and formed the basis for a stage play, a film, and a BBC Classic Serial. Since the day they were first published Anne Frank's diaries have never been out of print. Today the "secret annexe" in the

Prinsengracht is a museum and a shrine, visited by thousands of young people every year.

Intelligent and artistic as she was, Anne Frank was still an ordinary young girl who loved her family and her friends and kept a secret diary. An ordinary young girl who died in squalor and misery in her sixteenth year, caught up in humanity's greatest crime. Just one of six million.

CHAPTER 6
SUPERNATURAL HORROR

After the all-too-real atrocities carried out by mankind, it's almost a relief to turn back to the dark shadows of the supernatural world.

Vampires

Of all the horrors that have haunted the imagination, one of the most powerful and long-lasting is the vampire. Vampires have been around for a very long time. In ancient Greece they were mostly female – beautiful women who waylaid lonely travellers, led them astray and then drained their blood. According to Jewish folklore, Lilith, Adam's first wife, was a vampire, who attacked sleeping men, draining their blood. She even had a gang of followers, the Lillim, who went around doing the same thing. The Assyrians, the Chinese, and even the American Indians have vampire legends of their own. The American Indians have a particularly nasty one – a vampire with a trumpet-shaped mouth who sucks its victims brains out through their ears!

Vlad the Impaler

In Europe, vampires tend to be linked with real-life monsters – like Gilles de Rais, whom we dealt with earlier. One of the most infamous was Vlad Tepesh, the original Count Dracula, a name much associated with vampire lore. The count, who eventually became King Vlad IV of Transylvania, was a fifteenth-century ruler who won many victories against the invading Turks. Vlad had the unpleasant habit of impaling his enemies on sharpened stakes. He specialized in mass executions, and after capturing an enemy

Vlad The Impaler

town, impaled most of the inhabitants and sat down to dine in the middle of his dying victims. When one of his own noblemen complained that being surrounded by the dead and dying was spoiling his dinner, Vlad had him impaled as well. In deference to the man's rank, Vlad provided him with a longer stake, so that his dying body was raised up above the others.

Vlad is reputed to have executed between 30 000 to 100 000 people during his reign. Eventually he was defeated, captured, and beheaded by the Turks.

Bloody Elizabeth

Amongst Vlad's supporters was Prince Stephen Bathory, which provides a link to another human, or rather inhuman, monster. One of Prince Stephen's descendants was Countess Elizabeth Bathory, who lived in traditional vampire territory, on the edge of the Carpathian mountains.

The countess was obsessed with the idea of perpetual youth. In order to achieve this aim, she kidnapped young peasant girls from the surrounding countryside, slit their throats, drained their blood into huge vats and bathed in it. By soaking herself frequently in young fresh blood, she believed she could stay young and beautiful for ever.

As with Gilles de Rais, the countess came to a sticky end. One of her intended victims escaped and rumours of the countess's crimes began spreading throughout Hungary. They reached the ears of the king himself, who sent soldiers to investigate the goings-on at the countess's gloomy and forbidding castle. When they discovered the dead bodies of young girls and the blood-filled vats, the horrified king ordered the countess to be put to death.

In 1610, Countess Elizabeth Bathory was walled up in her own bedchamber, and left there to die.

Vampire Village

In 1732, when much of the Balkans formed part of the Austrian Empire, an Austrian medical officer was given an unusual assignment. Reports had been reaching the authorities that a village near Belgrade was being plagued by vampires. The medical officer was ordered to take a team and make a thorough investigation. His official report still survives today, witnessed and signed by the officer and his four assistants.

When he and his staff arrived, the villagers told them that some time ago a villager had broken his neck in a fall. In the years before he died, this particular villager had often spoken about being attacked by a vampire.

Soon after the villager's death, several people in the village became the victims of a vampire. Three of them died. So, the village leaders dug up the original villager and found that his body was fresh and undecayed, with fresh blood flowing from eyes, mouth and ears. Convinced that he was a vampire they drove a stake through his heart. The body groaned and blood flowed from the wound. The villagers burned the body to ashes, scattering them on the grave.

For a time all had been well – but now the vampires had returned. The villagers said that the original vampire had attacked cattle as well as humans. Other villagers had eaten the tainted flesh and the infection had spread – a sort of mad vampire disease.

The medical officer went to the village cemetery and supervised the digging up of the suspected graves. About a dozen bodies were found in what he describes in his report as "a condition of vampirism" – the bodies fresh and healthy-looking, and filled with fresh blood.

All the vampire bodies had their heads cut off and were burned to ashes, which were scattered over the river.

Vampires of the Balkans

For a long time the vampire remained a creature of Eastern Europe. In 1746 a contemporary chronicler wrote: "Hungary, Moravia, Silesia, and Poland are the principal theatre of these happenings. For here we are told that dead men, men who have been dead for several months, I say, return from the tomb, are heard to speak, walk about, infest hamlets and villages, injure both men and animals, whose blood they drain, making them sick and ill and at length actually causing death."

The old chronicler gives a number of methods of dealing with the vampire problem. "Nor can men deliver themselves from these terrible visitations, nor secure themselves from these horrid attacks, unless they dig the corpses up from the graves, drive a sharp stake through these bodies, cut off the heads, tear out the hearts, or burn the bodies to ashes. The name given to these ghosts is Oupires, or Vampires, that is to say, bloodsuckers . . ."

Literary Vampires

From the very beginning, vampires proved popular with horror writers and their readers. One of the first vampire stories has an impressive literary pedigree.

One evening in 1816, the English poet Lord Byron, fellow-poet Shelley, Mary, Shelley's beautiful young wife, and John Polidori, Byron's doctor, decided to have a spooky story competition.

Polidori's contribution was a story, called *The Vampyre*. Today it's reckoned to be rather a feeble effort. (Surprisingly, the shy and gentle Mary Shelley was a clear winner with her story *Frankenstein*. The megalomaniac, life-creating scientist and his mixed-up monster were later to star in almost as many movies as Count Dracula himself.)

The vampire tradition continued with a popular Victorian potboiler called *Varney the Vampire, or The Feast of Blood*. Written in an amazing 220 chapters by some anonymous but undeniably hardworking hack, it tells of the diabolical deeds of aristocratic vampire Sir Francis Varney. A handsome figure with blazing eyes and sharp teeth, Varney is a seductive, upper-class vampire. This was soon to become an established tradition.

In 1870 the vampire story took a decidedly

glamorous turn with "Carmilla" *In a Glass Darkly*, by Victorian horror-writer Sheridan Le Fanu. Decidedly the best vampire story so far, "Carmilla" is the terrifying tale of a beautiful lady vampire with the useful ability to turn herself into a giant cat.

Just like handsome but diabolical aristocrats, seductive lady vampires were to become a recognized feature of the vampire genre. In fact, for reasons that might well baffle Freud, modern-day vampires have always been considered extremely sexy.

The most famous vampire of all was created by a writer called Bram Stoker. A cheerful, good-natured Irishman, Stoker spent his days working as stage-manager to Sir Henry Irving, the greatest actor of the day. But there was a darker side to Stoker, and it found relief in writing a series of horror stories in the little spare time he had. The stories, in the style of Le Fanu, or Edgar Allan Poe, featured such gruesome incidents as a man who buries his murdered mistress under his house, only to find her long golden hair growing up through the floorboards. In another of Stoker's stories, *The Judge's House*, a notorious hanging judge returns as a giant rat after his death.

In 1897 Stoker wrote the story which made him famous, the only one of his works still remembered today. He called his vampire Count Dracula, one of the many titles borne by the appalling Vlad the Impaler. But in all other respects, Stoker's Dracula is very different. The Count Dracula of the novel is a suave European nobleman with the white face, burning eyes, and long black cloak that have formed the vampire image ever since.

Dracula is rather hard going for the modern reader. The story is told in the then-popular "epistolary" form – a series of letters and journals. It begins with the diary of Jonathan Harker, a young English estate agent. (*Dracula* must be the only novel with an estate agent hero.) Harker is sent from London to Transylvania with the deeds of an English country house which Count Dracula, a wealthy Transylvanian nobleman is interested in buying.

After a long journey through the wild and beautiful Transylvanian countryside, Harker arrives, at midnight, at Castle Dracula, and is greeted by the count himself: "His hand grasped mine with a strength which made me wince, an effect which was not lessened by the

A Stake to the Heart

fact that it seemed cold as ice, more like the hand of a dead than a living man." Harker also notices that the count has red lips and long sharp teeth, and that his nails are filed to sharp points.

The count insists that Harker stays at Castle Dracula as his guest while he studies the papers. The atmosphere is sinister in the

extreme. The castle is kept locked and Harker is a prisoner. Very soon he starts wondering if he'll ever get out alive.

Looking out of the window at night, Harker sees Dracula climbing down the castle walls, head downwards, like a giant bat. Soon after Harker has an unnerving encounter with three ladies, who want to give him "vampire kisses". He is only saved by the arrival of Dracula himself, who still has a use for him. Exploring the castle by day, Harker finds Dracula in his coffin. "There lay the Count . . . on the lips were gouts of fresh blood which trickled from the corners of the mouth and ran over the chin and neck . . . It seemed as if the whole awful creature were simply gorged with blood."

That night Dracula's coffin is carried away by his servants and Jonathan is left alone in the castle – with the three bloodthirsty vampire ladies. He decides to climb down the castle walls and escape . . .

The story moves to England, where Dracula is trying to get his fangs into Harker's fiancée Minna and her friend Lucy. Opposing him are the novel's three young heroes. Arthur Holmwood, Quincey Morris, a young Texan, and Dr John Seward, who runs the local asylum. All three of them are in love with Lucy.

They are aided by wise old Professor Van Helsing, a visiting vampire expert.

Dracula has his evil way with Lucy. He sucks her blood until she dies – or rather she becomes one of the un-dead, a vampire, roaming the countryside at night, attacking children and sucking their blood.

Van Helsing and our three heroes open her coffin. They find Lucy with blood on her lips, looking healthier than when she died.

Reluctantly they take the necessary steps...

"Arthur took the stake and the hammer...placed the point over the heart... Then he struck with all his might. The Thing in the coffin writhed and a hideous, blood-curdling scream came from the opened red lips. The body shook and quivered and twisted in wild contortions; the sharp white teeth champed together till the lips were cut and the mouth was smeared with

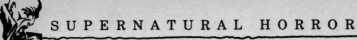

a crimson foam . . . And then the writing and quivering of the body became less, and the teeth seemed to champ and the face to quiver. Finally it lay still. The terrible task was over. There in the coffin lay no longer the foul Thing . . . but Lucy as we had seen her in life, with her face of unequalled sweetness and purity . . . The Professor and I sawed the top off the stake, leaving the point of it in the body. Then we cut off the head, and filled the mouth with garlic. We soldered up the leaden coffin, screwed on the coffin-lid and gathering up our belongings we came away."

Van Helsing and the three young men swear to find Dracula and destroy him. The trail

takes them around London, across Europe, and finally to Castle Dracula itself, where Dracula gets the sharp stake and beheading treatment. Dracula may be dead, but in true vampire fashion he refuses to lie down. The novel was an immediate best-seller, and has never been out of print since its publication. Over the years it has been translated into almost every language.

It took the coming of the movies to give Count Dracula true immortality. The first, and one of the the most artistic films was an unauthorised silent version called *Nosferatu* filmed by the great German director Murnau. Avoiding the suave image, the actor Max Schreck played Dracula as a semi-human monster, a bald, rat-like figure with huge fangs and talons.

Dracula's next interpreter was Bela Lugosi in several black-and-white talkies made in the thirties and forties. Lugosi's performance, all satanic sneers, swirling cloak and thick Hungarian accent, seems over the top today but he was hugely popular at the time.

Dracula really took off with the coming of colour – at last you could really get full value out of the blood! In 1957 Hammer, a small-scale British film company, had an unexpected success with their horror film *The Curse of Frankenstein*, with the monster played by an immensely tall actor called Christopher Lee. They decided to follow up with a remake of *Dracula,* with Christopher Lee as the count.

Thanks to Lee's terrifying Dracula, and an impressive Professor Van Helsing from Peter Cushing, the film was a tremendous hit. It was so successful that it spawned numerous sequels, few of them as good as the first. Christopher Lee got stuck with the cloak and the fangs for so long that he got thoroughly sick of them.

Even after the eventual decline of the Hammer Horror cycle, the vampires stayed with us. In *Salem's Lot*, horror writer Stephen King brought vampires to a small American town in the present day. When the book became a TV mini-series, the director, Tobe Hooper, reverted to a *Nosferatu*-style monster for the king vampire, although James Mason as the vampire's suave henchman keeps up the Dracula tradition.

Best-selling American author Anne Rice has had a huge success with her series of novels about a handsome and seductive vampire called Lestat. The first of these, *Interview with the Vampire* was recently filmed with Tom Cruise as Lestat.

The vampire is the most successful of all the supernatural monsters, and the fascination continues. It's interesting to see how the vampire made the change from monster to sex-symbol. Early vampires were little more than rotting corpses, climbing out of their graves to feed on the living. Today's vampires are more likely to be young and glamorous – and above all, sexy. Something about the combination of blood, death and sex seems to appeal to our deepest, darkest instincts . . .

What about the Werewolf?

Werewolves have never achieved quite the same popular appeal as vampires, although their legend is equally widespread. "Were" is old English for "man" and the phenomenon is by no means confined to wolves. Legends abound in many cultures of were-cats, were-tigers, and were-animals of almost every kind. The legend merges with the stories of shape-shifters – magicians, sorcerers, or sometimes simply accursed beings, who have the power to change themselves into bird or animals.

The werewolf legend in Europe seems to pre-date that of the vampire. In France in the hundred years between the early sixteenth and seventeenth centuries, there were thousands of reports of werewolves, or *loups-garous* as the French call them.

One typical report tells of a sixteen-year-old boy found dying of a stab wound. Before he

died he told those who found him that he had
been attacked by a wolf-like creature. When
he tried to drive it away with his knife, the
wolf had snatched the weapon with human-
like hands and stabbed him.

After the boy died a search was made of the
area and a simple-minded girl called Pernette
was found wandering nearby. The angry
townspeople decided she was a werewolf and
killed her. They then arrested her brother,
whose body was covered with scratches. They
also arrested his other sister, and his son.

When in jail, they started running about
their cell on all fours. At their trial all three
confessed to being werewolves. They said they
turned themselves into wolves by means of a
magic salve or ointment, given them by a
witch. They were sentenced to death and
burned at the stake.

The Werewolf of Cologne

Another story tells of wolf attacks on several
children in the Cologne area. After a child was
killed, local hunters tracked down a wolf. As
they approached the wolf, it vanished, and
instead the hunters found a man in the area of
woods where the wolf had disappeared. This
man was arrested and confessed to being a were-

wolf. He said that he had killed many children over the years as well as sheep and lambs. He too was found guilty of being a werewolf. He was broken on the wheel, and his head was cut off as well. Just to be on the safe side, his sister and his daughter were executed as well.

Werewolves in France

Another celebrated case occurred in Besançon in 1521, where two men, Pierre Bourgot and Michel Verdung were accused of being were-wolves. According to Bourgot's confession,

Verdung took him one night to a witches'
sabbath in a wood, where devil worshippers
were dancing, each carrying a green taper
with a blue flame. Bourgot described what
happened next: "After I had stripped myself he
smeared me with a salve and I believed myself
then to be transformed into a wolf. I was at
first somewhat horrified at my four wolf's feet
and the fur with which I was covered all at
once, but I found that I could now travel with
the speed of the wind."

Verdung too transformed himself into a wolf,
and the two went on a killing rampage
throughout the countryside. This wolf-run was
only the first of many.

On one occasion they tore to pieces a woman
gathering peas in the fields. On another they
devoured a little girl, all except one arm.
Verdung said her flesh tasted delicious. They
attacked and devoured other girls. Once with
no human victims around, they had to be con-
tent with a goat. After giving this damning
evidence, both men were executed.

In 1573 the region of Dole was being terror-
ized by werewolves, and the local peasants
were given special permission to carry arms
and hunt them down.

One evening some peasants were returning
from work in the fields when they heard the

screams of a child and the howling of a wolf coming from the forest. Running towards the sound, they saw a little girl trying to fight off a wolf-like creature, which had already wounded her several times. As the peasants came up the creature ran off into the woods. It was too dark to see much, but some of the peasants were convinced that they had recognized the features of the local hermit – a grim and surly man called Gilles Garnier, who lived in a hovel near St Bonnot.

Gilles Garnier was arrested and brought to trial. He confessed to being a werewolf and to having carried out attacks on a number of victims in the preceding months. In his wolf shape he had attacked a girl of twelve and devoured most of her body. On another occasion he had seized another girl, but three people had come up, and he had been forced to flee. A mile from Dole he had attacked and partially devoured a ten-year-old boy. Later he had killed a thirteen-year-old boy near Perrouze, but had been driven away before he could eat him.

As with other werewolves, Gilles' preferred victims seem to have been children. Whether this is because they made easier victims, or simply because they tasted better, isn't clear.

The Werewolf of Caude

In 1598, in wild and desolate country near Caude, some peasants found two wolves tearing at the mutilated bloody body of a young man. When the men approached the wolves ran away into the woods. Though the peasants followed their tracks, they eventually lost them. Soon afterwards they came upon a man crouched amongst the bushes. He was half-naked with long hair, a long beard and long sharp finger-nails. His hands were caked with blood. He was identified as a beggar called Roulet, who had recently been given food and shelter in a nearby village. Since then he had been missing for about a week.

Brought before the judge, Roulet, like most werewolves, made a full confession. Together with two other werewolves, he had killed the young man and started eating him, fleeing when the peasants arrived. Asked about the other two werewolves, Roulet said were his brother Jean and his cousin Julien. Roulet said he had been given an ointment by his parents, which enabled him to transform himself into a wolf. "Do your hands and feet become paws of a wolf?" asked the judge. "Yes, they do." "Does your head become like that of a wolf – your mouth become larger?" "I do not know how my head was at the time; I used my teeth. . . I have wounded and eaten many other little children."

On investigation it was proved that Roulet's brother Jean and and his cousin Julien had been some way away at the time of the attack. His parents, although poor, were good, respectable people.

Inevitably, Roulet was sentenced to death — but he appealed to the Parliament of Paris. Considering the usual harshness of the law in those times, the response was surprisingly liberal. The higher court decided that Roulet was mad rather than wicked. His death sentence was repealed and instead he was ordered to spend two years in the asylum at St-Germain-des Prés, "That he might be instructed in the knowledge of God, whom he had forgotten in his extreme poverty."

Literally thousands of werewolf attacks were reported in France at the time. Either there was a werewolf epidemic, or a sort of copycat effect led savage and mentally unbalanced men to commit so many terrible crimes.

Werewolves were always allied to witchcraft, and many report attending witches' sabbaths,

and being given a mysterious salve or ointment which enabled them to change shape. It
has been suggested that this ointment, rubbed
on all over, contained some kind of drug which
gave its users delusions of changing shape,
and inflamed them into committing their savage murders. The only other explanation, of
course, is that they were werewolves. . .

The myth of the werewolf is dark and savage, with none of the seductive glamour of the
vampire. Rather than being concerned with
handsome black-cloaked counts bending over
trembling maidens, werewolf tales are about
poor peasant children, torn to pieces in the
dark and gloomy woods of medieval France.

Werewolves on Film

Perhaps for this reason, the werewolf, although
extremely common in folklore all over the world,
is much rarer in fiction and on film. The most
famous werewolf novel is Guy Endore's *The
Werewolf of Paris*, published in 1933. There are
only a handful of werewolf movies. In the 1961
Curse of the Werewolf, based on Endore's novel,
the werewolf was played by a young Oliver Reed!

In Hollywood, actor Lon Chaney specialized
in werewolf roles. In films like the 1941
version, *The Wolf Man*, Chaney's werewolf is
a sad, even pathetic character. He is a man

under a curse, only too anxious to get rid of his bad habit of turning into a wolf at the time of the full moon.

One recent werewolf movie of note was the 1981 *An American Werewolf in London*, a black comedy with truly astonishing werewolf special effects.

The Wonderful World of Witches

Unless you are extremely unlucky, you are unlikely to bump into a werewolf or a vampire.

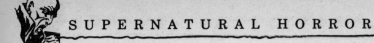

But you might very easily meet a witch. There might be one living next door, or in the next street. Today, under its ancient name of "Wicca" or the Old Religion, witchcraft has become quite respectable. Yet it was very different in the bad old days . . .

The trouble with witches is that almost anyone might be one. Even in historical times you had to indulge in some pretty eccentric behaviour to be suspected of being a werewolf or a vampire. But almost any woman could be accused of being a witch. Many were – and many died because of it.

Although stories of vampires and werewolves originated in distinct areas of Europe, witches seem to be found in a wider variety of locations. There are plenty of reports of witchcraft from other countries of course, but witches do seem to have thrived particularly well in the British Isles.

The Witches' Sabbath

Traditionally witches are worshippers of Satan. They operate as part of a coven, a group of thirteen, usually with a man as the leader. Witches are generally thought of as being female, although strictly speaking witch is a unisex word. (The specifically male version, "warlock", is far less common.)

At the witches' service, the Black Mass, the candles are black and the cross above the altar is upside down. The service features chanting, drinking, naked dancing, and the magic ointment or salve that crops up so often in the werewolf tales. As has been suggested, the salve may have contained some kind of drug which enabled the witches to fly – or to think they were flying – through the night skies on the traditional broomstick.

One of the aims of the service was to summon up the Devil in person, so that his disciples could worship him. If he condescended to turn up at all, the Evil One usually appeared in the form of a giant black goat. The Black Mass ended in what Victorian writers used to call "nameless orgies".

The sacrifice of children was thought to be an essential part of witchcraft. According to Reginald Scot, a sixteenth-century writer on the subject of witchcraft, witches had a quota: every witch was expected to kill a child every fortnight – or at the very least, one a month. It is therefore interesting to note that in 1645 a witch called Mary Johnson was executed at Wivenhoe in Essex for poisoning two children in an act of witchcraft.

The Church believed in witchcraft, and was

The Witchfinder

eager to stamp it out. In the seventeenth century self-appointed witchfinders went about the country, tracking the devil-worshippers down. One of the most famous – or infamous – was a man called Matthew Hopkins, who was known as the Witchfinder-general. Hopkins had a whole range of cruel methods for proving the guilt of a suspected witch. For instance, a witch was "walked" between two inquisitors, kept moving and deprived of food and sleep for twenty-four hours. Or instead she might be "cross-bound" right toe to left thumb, left toe to right thumb, sat on a high stool and watched for twenty-four hours. This was to see if her familiars, or servant imps and demons, came to feed from her, perhaps in the form of flies, mice or spiders. The most usual witch's familiar, of course, was her cat. Traditionally the witch's cat was black, but not always. At a trial in Chelmsford, a witch confessed that her familiar was a white-spotted cat called Satan, given to her by her grandmother, herself a notorious witch. Her grandmother had taught her that every time she asked the cat to do anything for her she must feed it with bread and milk and a drop of her own blood.

Matthew Hopkins would order the witch's body to be searched for a "witchmark", an extra nipple with which she fed her familiars. The witchmark however, could also be disguised as any ordinary mole or birthmark. To make sure, a long needle was run into the mole. If it was really a witchmark, the witch would feel no pain.

If all else failed, Hopkins had one final, infallible method. The witch, still cross-bound,

was taken to the village pond and "swum" — thrown into the water. Since water was the sacred element used in holy baptism it naturally refused to accept anything as evil as a witch. So, if the witch floated, as most bodies will, that was sure proof of her guilt. She was taken out of the pond and either hanged or burned at the stake. Hopkins, like other witch-hunters, was fond of quoting the relevant text in the Bible, Exodus 22:18, "Thou shalt not suffer a witch to live."

If the poor woman sank, on the other hand, she was innocent. Of course, she was probably drowned as well . . .

A man in love with his work, Matthew Hopkins is said to have been responsible, by these dubious methods, for the execution of

200 witches in the eastern counties of England. He charged a modest fee of twenty shillings per town or village.

There's a sort of poetic justice in Hopkins' final fate. In 1647 he published a book, *The Discovery of Witches*. That same year he was accused of being a witch himself. He was tried, found guilty and hanged.

Scottish Witches

Scotland provides many stories of witchcraft. A Scottish writer who studied the subject said it was ironic that "the Land of the Lord should be the favourite camping ground of Satan".

In 1590 a coven of Scottish witches, led by a sorcerer called Doctor Faen, plotted against the life of King James I who had been very active against witchcraft. When King James and Queen Anne were returning from a voyage to Denmark, members of the coven christened a cat – this act of blasphemy was part of a powerful black magic ceremony. They tied parts of a dismembered corpse to the unfortunate animal and took it out to sea – sailing of course in their sieves, the traditional form of marine transport for witches. Amid much chanting of spells the unfortunate cat was cast into the water. This done, "Then did arise such a tempest in the sea, as a greater has not been seen."

Meanwhile the royal fleet was sailing peacefully homewards. A sudden storm sprang up, directed exclusively against the king's own ship. All the other vessels enjoyed following winds.

Only the king's ship had to struggle against the storm all the way back to Scotland. He was lucky to get back alive. One of the witches confessed the plot when Doctor Faen and his coven were arrested and put on trial. According to her, it was only King James' exceptional religious piety that saved him: "The witch declared that his majesty had never come safe from the sea if his faith had not prevailed above their

intentions."

Not all witches' spells had so exalted a target. At Dornoch in Sutherland in 1722, an old woman was burned for bewitching her neighbour's cattle. She was the last witch to be executed in Scotland.

Although witchcraft trials and burnings at the stake are a thing of the past, witchcraft itself survived into modern times, enjoying something of a revival in the thirties and forties.

In 1940 when England faced the threat of German invasion, witches called a Great Coven, a sort of mass rally of witches, in the New Forest. There they set up the Great Circle – a magic ritual used at the time of the Spanish Armada (which was only defeated with the help of a great storm) and in 1800 when Napoleon threatened invasion. The patriotic witches sent a wave of psychic power across the sea to Hitler, bearing the command, "You cannot cross the sea. You cannot come."

The ceremony eventually had to be suspended. Apparently it was so powerful that several of the older witches died. Still, it obviously worked. Perhaps Hitler got to hear of it and it put him off. He would certainly have taken it seriously as the Nazis were firm believers in black magic and spent a great deal of time and money studying the occult.

Present-day witchcraft takes on a more benevolent form, with good or "white" witches in the ascendant. White magic can be us ed for healing rather than for cursing. Since witchcraft has always represented a primarily female power, it has been endorsed by some members of the feminist movement. In America, a modern witch has launched her own cable TV station offering courses in elementary Wicca . . .

CHAPTER 7

HORRORS FROM SPACE

We turn now from the horrors of Earth, both natural and supernatural, to the greatest mysteries of all – the unknown terrors of space. The universe is so vast, with so many millions of planets, that it seems impossible that Earth is the only one with intelligent life. But if there are intelligent aliens somewhere out there, they've certainly been carrying on in some very strange ways . . .

UFOs and Little Green Men

UFOs – Unidentified Flying Objects – go back a lot further than you might think. One of the earliest UFOs was reported in Denison, Texas in 1878. A farmer working in his fields reported seeing a disc-shaped object moving across the clear sky.

He told a reporter from the local paper that it moved "at a wonderful speed" and looked like a saucer skimming across the sky. This is probably the first report of a mysterious saucer-shaped something in the sky. There were many more to come.

Foo Fighters

During the Second World War Allied pilots

reported strange glowing balls which floated past and sometimes actually *through* their planes. For some reason they called them "Foo Fighters". The English and American pilots believed that the glowing balls might be some kind of German or Japanese secret weapon – perhaps part of a new surveillance system since they never did any real harm.

After the war it was discovered that German and Japanese pilots had been harassed by the glowing balls as well – and were convinced that they were the work of the English or Americans!

The First Sighting

The man usually credited with beginning the post-war UFO craze is Kenneth Arnold, a business man who flew his own private plane.

On 24 June 1947, Arnold was flying solo from Chehalis to Yakima in Washington State. He had heard reports that a US Marine Corps transport plane had crashed in the Mount Rainier area, and that there was a $5000 reward for finding the wreckage. Mount Rainier wasn't too far off Arnold's homeward route, and the $5000 would certainly come in handy. He decided it was worth taking a look.

As he reached Mount Rainier, he suddenly

saw a flash of light. Just north of Mount Rainier nine strangely-shaped craft were flying in a line. At first he thought they were simply aeroplanes – then he realized that the craft were round with no sign of wings or tail-formations. Arnold estimated that the strange craft were about twenty-five miles away, and that each one was about the size of an airliner. He calculated that they must be moving at well over 1000 miles an hour – an impossible speed for any aeroplane of the time.

Arnold decided to report what he'd seen to the FBI. (He might have been included in one of the early X-Files!) By the time he landed at Yakima their office was closed. He told his friends amongst the other pilots what he'd seen, and flew on to his next destination, Pendleton, Oregon. Meanwhile the press picked up the story. By the time he landed at Pendleton, a crowd of newspapermen was waiting to interview him. Kenneth Arnold wasn't some wandering eccentric. He was an established business man and an experienced pilot, so his report carried conviction. The story went out all over the world. What's more, it provoked hundreds of other reports from people claiming to have seen very much the same thing.

"If I was to go by the number of reports,"

said Arnold wryly, "I thought that it wouldn't be long before there was one of these things in every garage!" Continually besieged by journalists keen for fresh details, and annoyed by newspaper stories accusing him of being either a deluded fool or a deliberate hoaxer, Arnold decided it was all a waste of time. He got in his plane and flew back home to Boise, Idaho, wanting only to forget the whole thing.

But the story refused to die. Newspapers were being snowed under with reports of UFO sightings. A reporter christened them "flying saucers" and somehow the name stuck...

The Roswell Incident

The next major UFO incident happened only a few weeks after the Arnold sightings. A sheep farmer in New Mexico heard a tremendous explosion during the night. Next day he drove out to investigate, and found an area strewn with some strange material. It was metal-like, but it wasn't metal. You couldn't cut or break it. Twisted and distorted, it sprang back to its original shape. It was as light as balsa wood, and some of the larger pieces were marked with strange symbols. The farmer had read the flying saucer stories currently filling the papers, and decided he ought to report his find. He told the local sheriff's office and they passed the report on to the local US Air Base at Roswell.

The US Air Force sent an intelligence officer in a jeep. He studied the site, collected some of the strange metallic material and took his finds back to the base for study. Next day the Air Base issued an official press release. The remains of a crashed flying saucer had been discovered just outside Roswell.

Coming so soon after the Arnold sighting, and all the others that had followed, the story caused an enormous sensation. Journalists besieged the Air Base and fast-growing stories of the "captured UFO" spread out all over the world. Faced with something very like a nation-wide panic, the authorities seemed to panic themselves. The first steps of what looked like a massive cover-up were put into operation.

An Air Force general issued a second official statement saying that the original press release was a mistake. The fragments were simply those of a weather balloon. The intelligence officer who had collected the original fragments was sent for and told to keep his mouth shut about the entire incident for reasons of national security. He was ordered to pose for the press with fragments of an actual weather balloon. Years later, he said that this material had been specially substituted for the occasion by higher authorities, and was nothing like the actual material that he had found. The sheep farmer who had found the original mysterious fragments was taken into custody in Roswell Air Base and detained there for several weeks, under a kind of informal arrest. (He said later he hadn't actually been arrested, he just hadn't been allowed to leave.) Everyone else involved in the incident was warned to keep silent, now and in the future. Only one reason was given for all the secrecy – national security.

Inevitably the cover-up failed to work. In fact, it is at this point that the "conspiracy theory" side of the UFO phenomenon was born. Today many Ufologists, as students of, and believers in, the UFO phenomenon are called, are quite convinced that flying saucers are alien spacecraft. In the States, as elsewhere, they think that their government knows this perfectly well, and is hiding the truth from honest citizens, no doubt for some highly sinister reasons. They believe that their government is in possession of a number of captured spacecraft, some of which they have already flown experimentally. They also believe that the authorities have the bodies, alive or dead, of alien astronauts. (That these beliefs are widely held, or at the very least widely sympathized with, can be seen from the success of the many UFO books over the years and the current amazing popularity of *The X-Files* television series.)

What is certain is that, at the time, the secretive behaviour of the authorities simply increased speculation, fuelling the public's belief that there really was something to hide. Stories leaked out that the US Air Force had found not just a few metallic fragments but the wreck of an entire alien craft. It was rumoured that the bodies of alien astronauts had been taken away for study, and that at least one of them was still alive . . .

Many years later a local man came out with a story that seemed to confirm these rumours. He had been out on the plains, some way from the Roswell site when he found the wreckage of "a disc-shaped craft". Beside it lay the dead bodies of four alien beings – skinny, slight creatures with large bald heads. Within min-

utes the military arrived. Sealing off the area, they told the man to stay out of the area, and to say nothing. Later, one more piece of evidence emerged. A woman who had been a typist at a nearby air base said she was given the job of typing up an autopsy report on the body of a dead alien being.

Nearly fifty years later, the Roswell story still won't go away. Books have been written about the Roswell incident, and a television documentary on the subject was screened not long ago.

As recently as 1994 the US Air Force came out with yet another unconvincing explanation. The fragments *did* come from a weather balloon – but from a new and, then, top-secret kind of weather balloon. Somehow nobody seems very convinced.

Friend or Foe

But if the UFOs were alien spacecraft, what were the aliens up to? Why were they observing us? Why didn't they make contact? Were they benevolent, hostile, or simply neutral?

The reports of UFO sightings continued to flood in. An Eastern Airlines pilot reported his plane being "buzzed" by a cigar-shaped craft which whizzed past and then vanished in a burst of flame. There were hundreds of such sightings in the following years. Frequently the strange objects showed up on radar screens as well. Pilots would report strange glowing objects, sometimes round, sometimes cigar-shaped, hovering around, or perhaps "buzzing" their aircraft, and then vanishing at incredible speed. Very often that was all that happened – as if the UFOs were simply curious. But eventually events seemed to be taking a more dangerous turn. People started to die.

In June 1948, state police in Madisonville, Kentucky, received numerous reports of something that looked like a giant UFO. It was heading towards Goodman Air Force Base, so they sent a warning to the commanding officer. A few minutes later a metallic cone-shaped object with a glowing crimson top was seen hovering over the base.

The commanding officer sent up three fighter planes to investigate. The object shot rapidly upwards, with the three fighters in pursuit. Two of them abandoned the chase, but the third hung on. Its pilot, Captain Mantell radioed that the "thing" was directly in front of him, moving at 360 miles an hour.

"I'll pursue it as high as 20 000 feet," said Captain Mantell. They were the last words anyone ever heard him speak.

The "thing" and the pursuing fighter climbed higher and higher, disappearing into the sky. No more was heard from Captain Mantell, and all radio contact was lost with his plane. It had simply vanished. A search was launched and the wreckage of the fighter was found, strewn over a three-mile area.

An official enquiry was held. Its eventual verdict was that Captain Mantell had been chasing "the light of the planet Venus", which

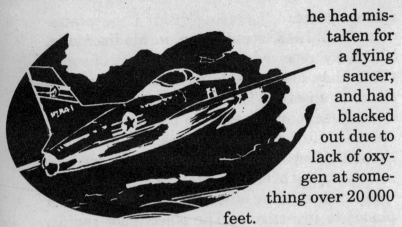

he had mistaken for a flying saucer, and had blacked out due to lack of oxygen at something over 20 000 feet.

The Navy later claimed that experimental reconnaissance balloons were being tested in the area. Ufologists, of course, saw things very differently. Clearly, Captain Mantell had chased a flying saucer, got too close, and had been shot down. Now the authorities were covering up, as usual. This was the first UFO fatality. It wasn't to be the last.

The McChord Mystery

In April 1959 a C-118 transport plane took off from the McChord Air Force Base, at Tacoma, Washington, on a routine training mission. The plane was tracked on the radar at the base. Suddenly the radar operators noticed that the C-118 was being followed by strange circles of light. There seemed to be three or four of the strange objects, hovering around the plane. Occasionally one would dart towards the plane, and then veer away again.

Suddenly there came a distress call from the plane: "Mayday! Mayday! We've hit something, or something has hit us . . . This is it! This is it!" The transmission cut off.

Reports came in that the plane had crashed into the side of a mountain in the Cascade range. The US Air Force sent crash crews to the scene and cordoned off the area with armed guards. Reporters and sightseers were turned away.

The crash teams discovered the remains of the aircraft scattered across the mountain side. They found the bodies of three of the four crew members buried deep into the ground by the impact of the crash. The body of the fourth man was never found.

Crash investigators discovered that the plane hadn't nose-dived as might have been expected. It had struck the mountain-side belly-first as though slammed down by some tremendous force.

Just before the crash, local residents had heard a series of tremendously loud explosions and had seen luminous objects in the sky, moving very fast and in complete silence.

Eyewitnesses to the crash had seen the C-118 appear overhead. Its engines seemed to have cut out, and part of the tail was missing. Three luminous shapes appeared to be chasing it. The plane and its strange pursuers disappeared from sight, and then there were two bright flashes in the sky.

The Vanishing Cessna

In October 1978 an Australian pilot called Frederick Valentich was flying his private plane, a little Cessna, from Melbourne to King Island, off the coast of Victoria. Over the Bass Strait he saw what he first thought was another aircraft. Then he realized that it was something very different.

Round and metallic, and glowing with green light, it buzzed his Cessna and then hovered above him. His engine started to falter.

Valentich contacted Melbourne Airport on his radio, and reported his situation. Asked what he planned to do Valentich replied, "My intentions are to go to King Island." Then he added, "That strange aircraft is hovering on top of me again. It is hovering, and it's not an aircraft . . ."

There was no further transmission. Frederick Valentich and his Cessna simply vanished, never to be seen again.

Close Encounters

It's astonishing to see a UFO flashing across the skies; it's alarming to find one following your plane – or your car; and there are hundreds of reports of such events occurring, with astronauts, pilots and policemen among the observers. They're what the Centre for UFO Studies calls Close Encounters of the First Kind – somebody sees something strange and that's all!

In Close Encounters of the Second Kind the strange object affects the environment in some way. Engines cut out, vegetation is scorched, landing marks are found. The Third Kind is when alien beings are seen. But some people have claimed to have closer, and far more uncomfortable encounters with UFOs which are known as Close Encounters of the Fourth Kind.

The Interrupted Journey

One evening in September 1966 a couple called Barney and Betty Hill were driving home after a trip to see Niagara Falls. They saw a light in the sky and got the impression it was following them. It came closer and closer and they were astonished to see an enormous disc, with two rows of windows, descending from the sky, and landing some way ahead.

Barney Hill stopped the car and went to take a closer look. Studying the strange craft through his binoculars, he could see alien shapes in some kind of uniform moving about behind the rows of windows.

He heard his wife calling from the car. "Barney, come back!" He turned and dashed back to the car, jumped in and started to drive away. Everything seemed strange and hazy, the car seemed to vibrate and he heard a soft beeping noise . . .

When the Hills got home they felt strange and out of sorts. Both their watches had stopped, and the journey home seemed to have taken far too long. Working out times and distances involved, the Hills reckoned they had "lost" two hours or more.

After the incident, Barney started to suffer from strange pains in his stomach and groin. He was afraid he might be suffering from radiation poisoning so he went to see a friend who was a physicist. Since the UFO incident some strange markings had appeared on the side of the Hills' car. The friend tested them with a geiger counter. The car was radioactive.

Betty meanwhile started having repeated nightmares about strange alien beings. Worried about their health, the Hills went to see a psychiatrist in Boston. During several months of hypnosis, he managed to recover the events of their missing hours.

Memories emerged of their abduction by the inhabitants of the flying saucer – small grey-skinned aliens with domed foreheads and slanting cat-like eyes. Betty remembered being given a thorough medical examination. The aliens took samples of her skin, hair and nails, and examined her from head to foot with strange scientific instruments. A needle was inserted into her navel and she screamed with pain. One of the aliens passed his hands in front of her face and the pain disappeared. Barney could remember much less, even under hypnosis, but he too remembered a medical examination.

When they were finally released, Barney and Betty now remembered they had strange feelings of peace and happiness. Barney recalled thinking, "We had nothing to fear."

They got back in the car and drove away, unaware of all that had happened to them – until the hypnosis brought it all back. A book about the Hills' experiences, *The Interrupted Journey* by John Fuller, became a best-seller in 1967.

The Hills were the first alien abductees to receive wide publicity, but there were to be many, many more. Over the years there have been hundreds and hundreds of abduction reports.

In October 1973, two shipyard workers called Hickson and Parker were enjoying a quiet bit of after-work fishing in the Pascuaga River, Mississippi.

A silvery craft suddenly descended from the skies and landed close by. A hatch opened and three aliens seemed to float out. They had grey skins, claw-like hands and a single eye.

Parker, who was only nineteen, was so scared he fainted dead away. Hickson said he was mysteriously paralysed and "floated" on board the craft. He was stretched on an operating table and some kind of electronic eye descended and examined him from head to foot. Then he found himself on the river bank again and the alien ship had disappeared.

The two men were so shaken that they rushed into the local police station and poured out the whole story. Not surprisingly, the sheriff was sceptical, and Hickson demanded to take a lie-detector test. The older of the two men, he was so distressed that he was in tears. The lie detector showed that Hickson certainly believed he was telling the truth.

The two maintained their story, even under hypnosis. The sheriff said later that they were just two country boys without the imagination to make up such a story. Professor Harder, a scientist who'd examined them, said, "The experience they went through was indeed a real one – a very strong feeling of terror impossible to fake under hypnosis. I've been left with the conclusion that we're dealing with an extra-terrestrial phenomenon."

One of the most famous alien abduction incidents took place in a national forest in Arizona on 5 November 1975.

Six young men, members of a forest wood-clearing team, were heading home in their truck after a day in the woods. Suddenly a UFO, large and golden with rows of windows, appeared, hovering in front of the truck at tree-top height. The driver stopped the truck and one of the party, a young man called Travis Walton, appeared to become hypnotised by the glowing shape. He jumped out of the truck and ran towards it. Horrified, his friends called to him to come back, but Travis took no notice. A blue ray came out of the glowing object and snatched him up.

The driver of the truck was so terrified that he started up the truck and put his foot down, speeding away. When they were well away from the scene the driver stopped the truck, and the five badly shaken young men discussed what to do. They decided they ought to go back and look for their friend. They found no sign of the UFO – but, although they searched all around, there was no sign of the missing Travis either. The five men went back to town and told their story. It was greeted with disbelief by the local inhabitants, and by the local law. The general opinion seemed to be that there had been some kind of quarrel out in the woods, and that one or more of the party had murdered Travis and hidden his body. Then they'd made up this unlikely story to explain his absence. During hours of questioning the five young men stuck to their story. The enquiry dragged on, with all five under a cloud of suspicion.

Several days later Travis Walton reappeared. He telephoned his sister from a phone booth several miles away. When she picked him up he was exhausted and shivering, grimy and unshaven and he had lost twenty pounds in weight. He didn't have the slightest idea where he'd been or what had happened to him.

Like Barney and Betty Hill, Travis Walton was treated with the technique called hypnotic regression to fill in the missing time. The memories that were revived were very much like those of the Hills.

Travis recalled running towards the spacecraft. "I was so excited as the truck stopped and I just jumped out and ran towards the glow. I felt no fear." Then something hit him. "Like an electronic blow to my jaw," said Travis. "Everything went black."

Travis woke up flat on his back on some kind of table. "I thought I was in hospital. I saw three figures. It was weird, they weren't human. They were about five feet tall and wore tight-fitting tan brown robes. Their skin was white like a mushroom but they had no clear features." Travis said he panicked and tried to escape. Then a man who seemed human appeared and took him to another room. Soon after that everything went black again.

"When I woke again I was shaky. I was on the highway. It was black but the trees were all lit up because just a few feet away was the flying saucer. I saw no one . . . I just ran." Realizing he was near a village not far from home, Travis found a phone booth and called his sister.

Travis's story was met with scepticism and suspicion – exactly as had happened with his friends. He took two lie-detector tests, failing one and passing the second. Travis took a long while to recover from his ordeal. "I wish it had never happened," he told his friends. "I don't enjoy being regarded as a liar."

Travis Walton's experiences became a best-selling book, and a film. Both were called *Fire in the Sky*. Everyone who has spoken to the six men concerned come away feeling that all six believe absolutely in their story. They have all maintained its truth for the last twenty years.

Alien encounters can be even closer than the ones described. In October 1957, a young Brazilian farmer called Antonio Villas-Boas had what you might call a Close Encounter of the Fifth Kind.

He was ploughing his fields when a shining, egg-shaped craft landed near him. Immediately his tractor engine cut out. Antonio tried to run, but small grey-uniformed humanoids emerged from the craft, caught him and dragged him inside. Once on board he

was stripped of his clothing, given a medical examination, and sponged with a freezing cold liquid.

The grey-uniformed humanoids went away, leaving Antonio alone. Another alien appeared, a female with soft blonde hair, a triangular face, large blue almond-shaped eyes and a pointed chin. Antonio said she was the most beautiful creature he had ever seen. She smiled down at him and put her arms around him. Antonio thought it only polite to respond to her advances, and they made love. "It was a normal act and she behaved like any other woman, even after repeated embraces. But she did not know how to kiss, unless her playful bites on my chin had the same meaning."

When it was all over the alien female went away, Antonio was returned to his field and the strange craft rose into the sky. Antonio told no one about his strange adventure – but he soon began to feel some very unpleasant after-effects. His eyes burned, he was unable to sleep and he felt continuously nauseous. Strange red marks appeared all over his body.

He went to see the local doctor who was baffled, and sent him on to a specialist in Rio de Janeiro. The specialist said Antonio was suffering from radiation poisoning. He had paid a high price for his few hours of alien passion.

Luckily Antonio recovered. He kept the whole story to himself, and only recounted it many years later, when he answered an appeal for UFO experiences. Another man, Howard Menger, also claimed to have encountered an attractive female alien. He married her.

More colourful, but less convincing, than most abduction stories, are those who claim to have communicated with aliens, gone for rides in their flying saucers, and even visited their home planets.

One of the first of these was a man called George Adamski, who started his career as a Ufologist selling hamburgers close to Mount Palomar Observatory. In his best-selling book *Flying Saucers Have Landed*, Adamski claimed to have met and talked with aliens in the California desert in 1952. Later he met aliens from from Mars, Venus, Jupiter and Saturn. Not only that, he had visited most of these planets himself in his alien friends' flying saucers. He also said the far side of the moon was now an alien base, a green and fertile spot with plants flourishing under protective domes.

In later years the achievements of the real-life space programme cast considerable doubt on most of Adamski's claims. However, for many years he was honoured by his many followers as the man the aliens had chosen to contact first as their Intergalactic Ambassador.

Ancient Aliens

Another UFO theory that has gained many followers is was that put forward by Erich Von Daniken and his disciples. According to him, UFOs, far from first appearing in the forties, have been visiting the Earth throughout history.

Indeed, even before history was recorded. Von Daniken believes that modern man was created from some primitive ape-like creature by alien-induced mutation, and the aliens have been visiting us ever since to share their wisdom. The subtitle of his book *Chariots of the Gods?* is *Was God an Astronaut?*

Von Daniken brings forward such evidence as:

Eighteenth-century Turkish maps so incredibly accurate they could only have been drawn with the aid of aerial photographs.

An immense pattern of lines and geometric shapes on the plains of Nazca in the Andes. Seen from the air, says Von Daniken, they suggest nothing so much as the ground-plan of a spaceport.

The legend of the ruined city of Tiahuanaco in Peru, which tells of a woman called Oryana who came in a golden spaceship from the stars and who had four webbed fingers. Rock drawings of four fingered beings survive in the city.

Glass-like pieces of rock called tektites, found in the Lebanon, which contain radioactive aluminium isotopes. A cave-drawing in the remote Asian region of Kohistan, correctly showing the exact position of the constellations 10 000 years ago – *with the Earth and Venus joined by a line*.

An engraving in an ancient Mayan Temple showing an astronaut-like figure surrounded by a tangle of immensely complex machinery.

Von Daniken links these and many other ancient marvels with today's UFOs, proving to his own satisfaction that aliens have always visited us – and are still doing so today!

The immense popularity of such Spielberg films as *Close Encounters of the Third Kind* and *ET*, and of spooky television shows from *The Twilight Zone* to *The X Files* proves the immense appeal of the strange, the terrifying and the unknown to the human mind.

So too does the fifty-year history of the UFO phenomenon. Whether the aliens, when and if they come, will be cute like ET, benevolent like those in *Close Encounters*, or ravenous predators like the one in *Alien* – well, there's no way of knowing. But if you should see a glowing light floating outside your window, approach with caution. You could be in for an uncomfortably close encounter of your own . . .

CHAPTER 8
HORRIBLY MYSTERIOUS

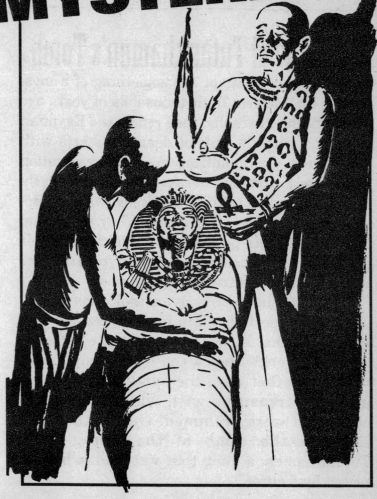

Some strange events seem to defy explanation. They just *are* – horrible mysteries that continue to puzzle and terrify us with their unknown menace. Here are a few of them.

The Curse of Tutankhamun's Tomb

The pyramids of Egypt are something of a mystery in themselves. Built thousands of years ago to glorify the Pharaohs, they reflect the Egyptian obsession with the cult of death. It starts with the process of mummification – the preservation of the body from the decay that follows death. But the Egyptian nobility didn't just want to preserve their bodies after death. They wanted to hang on to their power, their wealth, all their pomp and circumstance. An Egyptian ruler wanted to take his treasures with him.

The Egyptian noble even took slaves and servants – specially slain for the occasion – to make sure that he was properly looked after in the next world. Hence the immensely elaborate tombs that were the pyramids – and the amazing treasures with which the burial chambers were crammed. One of the richest was the tomb of the young King Tutankhamen; a tomb that was said to be protected by a curse . . .

Of course it had long been known that the tombs contained treasure. Over the years many had been broken into and robbed and the contents sold to unscrupulous collectors. It had long been recognized also that such sacrilegious grave robbing was unlucky.

The robbers risked bringing the wrath of the dead Pharaohs down on their heads. Only wicked or desperate men would take the risk.

There was of course another sort of person who wanted to break open the tombs. Egyptology, the study of Egypt's ancient civilization, had grown increasingly popular during the end of the nineteenth and the beginning of the twentieth centuries.

Respectable European archaeologists were eager to open the tombs, not just to find the treasure, but to study the relicts of Egypt's glorious past. But whatever the motives, the result was the same. The graves of the Pharaohs, sealed for thousands of years, were being broken into.

George Herbert, Lord Carnarvon, had no background in archaeology. He had originally come to Egypt in the hope that the dry air would be good for his breathing difficulties. But the subject was fashionable, and Lord Carnarvon became interested. He had the money to finance archaeological expeditions, and he allied himself with a famous archaeologist called Howard Carter. From 1907 onwards, Carter and Carnavon collaborated on a number of archaeological digs in the fabled Valley of the Kings, home of many of the most important tombs. Carnarvon provided the money, Carter the archaeological expertise.

Howard Carter made the archaeological discoveries he craved – such as the tombs of the Pharaohs Hatshepsut and Amenhotep I. Lord Carnarvon enjoyed the fame and glory their discoveries brought them, and they both enjoyed the congratulations of museums and fellow Egyptologists all over the world.

By 1923 they were on the trail of the biggest prize of all – the tomb of the boy-king Tutankhamun who had ascended the throne at the age of

twelve and died when
he was only eighteen.
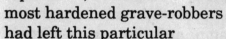
For a long time
the exact where-
abouts of the tomb
had been hidden
from European
archaeologists.
Because of its sinister
reputation, even the
most hardened grave-robbers
had left this particular
tomb alone. It had never been broken into and
the fabulous treasure inside was still intact.
But now Carter and Carnarvon had discovered
clues to the location of the tomb. They began
to prepare an expedition. It was to be Lord
Carnarvon's last.

Back in England making arrangements for
the expedition, Lord Carnarvon received a
strange message. It came from a certain Count
Hamon, a famous mystic of the day. The message read: "Lord Carnarvon do not enter tomb.
Disobey at peril. If ignored will suffer sickness. Not recover. Death will claim him in
Egypt."

Lord Carnarvon tried to shrug the warning
off. But he was sufficiently worried to visit two
other psychics. Both warned him of impending

danger. Having sought their advice Lord Carnarvon decided to ignore it. He just couldn't face giving up this last great achievement. Putting a brave face on it, he pooh-poohed the whole idea of a curse and went on with his preparations.

Lord Carnarvon returned to Egypt and the dig began. The site of the tomb – or at least, what they hoped was the site – was in the Valley of the Kings, near Luxor.

Rumours of the curse spread through the archaeologists' camp, and the local workmen were uneasy. Lord Carnarvon mocked their fears, still pouring public scorn on the idea of a curse. A fellow-archaeologist said, "If Carnarvon goes down into the tomb in that spirit, I don't give him long to live." Soon the workers found fragments bearing the name Tutankhamun. They were in the right place.

On 17 February 1923 Howard Carter and Lord Carnarvon prepared to enter the burial chamber of King Tutankhamun. A crowd of twenty archaeologists and fellow-workers clustered behind them. As the chamber was opened, for the first time in three thousand years, torches were held high and Howard Carter and Lord Carnarvon looked inside. Someone asked Carter what he could see. "Things," whispered Carter in awe.

"Wonderful things. . ." The tomb of King Tutankhamun, rich in treasure, was to become one of the most important archaeological monuments in the world. Howard Carter and Lord Carnarvon entered the tomb. In their excitement they omitted to read the inscription above the door. It said: "Death will come to those who disturb the sleep of the Pharaohs."

Inside the tomb Carter and Lord Carnarvon found treasures beyond anything they had imagined. There was gold, precious jewels —

Tutankhamun's Tomb

and the solid gold coffin of King Tutankhamun.

But Lord Carnarvon was not to live long to
enjoy his success. As work on the tomb went
on he began to fell unwell and had to return to
the Hotel Continental in Cairo, where he fell
ill with a mysterious wasting fever. "I feel like
hell," he said. On 5 April 1923, forty-seven
days after entering Tutankhamun's tomb,
Lord Carnarvon died. Cairo was struck by a
massive power failure minutes after he died.
"Everything went dark. We lit candles and
prayed," said his son, who became the new
Lord Carnarvon. Back in England, they later
learned, Lord Carnarvon's dog gave a sudden
howl of grief – and died that same day.

Lord Carnarvon's fever was caused by an
infected mosquito bite on his cheek. When the
golden coffin was finally opened, there was a
mark on King Tutankhamun's face – in the
same place.

Sad as Lord Carnarvon's death was, it takes
more than one corpse to make a curse. In
itself, it wasn't all that surprising. Egypt,
especially in those days, was a notoriously
unhealthy place for Europeans. Sudden deaths
from mysterious oriental diseases were not
uncommon. But there were more deaths to
come . . .

The first was that of Arthur Mace, a fellow archaeologist, and one of the senior members of the expedition. Mace was also staying at the Hotel Continental. Soon after Lord Carnarvon's death, Mace too fell ill, complaining of excessive tiredness. He went into a mysterious coma and suddenly died. The local doctors were baffled by his death.

George Gould, an old friend of Lord Carnarvon, was shocked to hear of his death. He decided to come to Egypt to see if there was anything he could do to help.

On the journey from the port to the hotel, Gould stopped off to visit his old friend's greatest discovery. He went into King Tutankhamen's burial chamber. Next day he collapsed and died.

Archibald Reid was the radiologist of the expedition. He had actually X-rayed King Tutankhamun's body, in an attempt to determine its exact age – an act some might have considered sacrilegious in itself. Reid began feeling symptoms of exhaustion and was sent back to England. He died soon afterwards.

Four months after the discovery of the tomb, Richard Bethell, Lord Carnarvon's personal secretary, died of a heart attack.

Joel Wool, a wealthy British business man visiting Egypt at the time, was one of the first allowed to visit the tomb. Soon afterwards he died of a mysterious fever.

Twenty people had attended the opening of Tutankhamun's tomb. Six years after the event, twelve of them were dead. After seven years only two of the original expedition were still alive. Other early deaths, linked in some way to the expedition were those of Lord Carnarvon's wife, and his half-brother. The main survivor of the curse, and in some ways the most unlikely, was Howard Carter the leader of the expedition. He died in 1939 at the age of 66.

Having cut such a swathe through the original offenders, you might have expected the curse to fade away. But it was not to b e. Its effects lingered on, though the death-rate showed signs of slowing down.

One of the first of the later victims was

Mohammed Ibrahim, Egypt's Director of Antiquities. In 1966 he was ordered by the Egyptian Government to arrange an exhibition of the Tutankhamun treasure in Paris.

Mohammed Ibrahim was against the idea. A firm believer in the power of the curse, he had had a dream warning him that he was doomed if the Tutankhamun treasure left Egypt. The Government wouldn't listen. After a final meeting in which he tried, and failed, to convince government officials to abandon the idea, Mohammed Ibrahim left the building, stepped out into a clear road and was knocked down and killed by a speeding car.

In 1972 Tutankhamun was on the move again. His golden death-mask was being crated up in Cairo to be sent to an exhibition at the British Museum. In charge of the operation was Dr Gamal Mehrez, successor to the unfortunate Mohammed Ibrahim as Director of Antiquities. Unlike Mohammed Ibrahim, Dr Mehrez wasn't afraid of the curse. "I more than anyone else in the world have been involved with the tombs and mummies of the Pharaohs and I am still alive," he said rather rashly. "I am living proof that all the tragedies associated with the Pharaohs are pure coincidence. I don't believe in the curse for one moment."

That evening Doctor Mehrez dropped dead. He was 52.

The Tutankhamun mask and other Tutankhamun relics were flown to England in an RAF Transport Command plane. The chief pilot and the chief engineer on the flight died of heart attacks within a few years. Both were fit men with no previous history of heart trouble. The chief technician kicked the box containing the relics and said, "I've just kicked the most expensive thing in the world." On a later flight, a ladder broke as he was getting out of the aircraft. He broke his leg – the kicking one – and it was in plaster for five months. All in all, he got off lightly.

Various attempts have been made to find some natural explanation for the Curse of Tutankhamun's Tomb. One of the most surprising was suggested by an Italian atomic scientist, Professor Louis Bulgarini, as early as 1949. According to Professor Bulgarini, the Egyptians may have used atomic radiation to protect their tombs. "The floors of the tombs could have been covered with uranium. Or the graves could have been finished with radio-active rock. Rock containing both gold and uranium was being mined in Egypt 3000 years ago."

It has also been suggested that the tomb

may have held some long-dormant bacteria, perhaps a mutant strain, activated by the opening of the tomb. Or perhaps the Egyptians coated their treasure with deadly poison.

By now millions of people have seen Tutankhamun's treasure in exhibitions all over the world, without any ill-effects. But we would all be be wise to treat King Tutankhamun's relics with respect – just in case the curse hasn't entirely worn off yet . . .

The Bermuda Triangle

Not only sacred religious objects but places can be cursed. Sometimes the curse extends to whole areas of the earth – or of the sea. One of the biggest and most baffling mystery zones is an area of the Atlantic defined by a line from Florida to Bermuda, from Bermuda to Puerto Rico, and from Puerto Rico back through the

Bahamas to Florida. It's called the Bermuda, or sometimes the Devil's, Triangle.

The Bermuda Triangle has an interesting geophysical feature. It's one of only two places on Earth where the compass needle points to true, rather than magnetic, north. Apparently this confuses fishes so much that they sometimes swim upside down. It's an area of deceptive calms and sudden storms, crossed by the powerful currents of the Gulf Stream.

None of this seems quite sufficient to explain the fact that over 140 ships and planes have vanished, and over 1000 lives have been lost in this one relatively small stretch of sea.

The seas around the area known as the Bermuda Triangle have had a strange and sinister reputation from the earliest times. Christopher Columbus sailed this way, on the voyage that led to the discovery of America. One night in 1492 his crew saw strange green lights moving about on the sea. In 1502 a fleet of Spanish ships laden with gold left Santo Domingo, bound for Spain. Somewhere on the way they vanished in an incredibly powerful freak storm. Only ten wrecks were found. Twenty-seven treasure ships vanished without trace.

An American sailing ship called the *Grampus* spent many years battling pirates and slavers in Caribbean waters. In 1843 she was ordered home to Charleston, South Carolina. She was sighted, homeward bound, on 3 March 1843 – and never seen again.

In 1880 the British frigate *Atlanta,* with a crew of 290 cadets, disappeared in the Triangle. Six ships of the Channel Fleet patrolled the area for six weeks and found no trace of the missing ship.

Even after the dangerous days of sail had passed, ships still weren't safe in the Bermuda Triangle. In March 1919, the USS *Nina*, one of the early steam tugs, set off from Norfolk Navy Yard in Virginia to Havana, Cuba, to assist in salvage work. She was sighted off Savannah, Georgia, heading south, and never seen again.

The *Nina* was the first steam-powered vessel to vanish – but not the last. Towards the end of the First World War, the US Navy supply vessel *Cyclops* was sailing from Barbados home to Norfolk, Virginia, with a crew of 390 and a cargo of manganese. The weather was clear and sunny and the seas were calm. The *Cyclops* was a 500-foot, 19 000 ton cargo ship, newly built. She was equipped with all the latest radio equipment, recently installed, and newly tested. Yet in March 1918 the *Cyclops* simply vanished from the ocean, without even a distress call. No wreckage was found.

Since the ship had disappeared in war time, enemy action was assumed to be the cause. Perhaps the *Cyclops* had struck a mine, or encountered an enemy cruiser and been sunk instantly. Soon, when the war was over, it was possible to check up on what had happened. It was discovered that there had been no mine-field, and no enemy vessel, anywhere in the area. The disappearance of the *Cyclops* is still unexplained.

Ships continued to vanish in a steady stream in the years between the wars. Ten disappeared in 1921 alone, and other years were almost as bad. Some of the missing ships can be accounted for by sudden storms, hurricanes and dangerous seas. Others are not so easily explained.

In 1925 a Japanese freighter *Raifuku Maru* met a mysterious fate a very long way from her home waters. Somewhere beyond the Bahamas she ran into trouble. But what? The freighter had time only to send one quick coded message. "Danger like dagger now. Come quick." The rest was silence – and the ship was never seen again. Nobody knows what the message means.

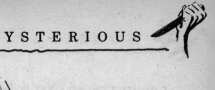

Lost in the Bermuda Triangle

Despite the area's long and sinister history, it wasn't until the end of the Second World War that the legend of the Bermuda Triangle really began. By now of course a new kind of voyager was risking the dangers of the Devil's Triangle, not sailing its treacherous seas but flying over them – at speeds far greater than any ship. But were they any safer?

In fact, quite a few aircraft vanished over the Triangle during the Second World War. But it wasn't until the war was nearly over that as many as five disappeared at once.

A group of seven bombers on their way to Italy stopped off to refuel in Bermuda. Soon after they set off again, they hit freak weather conditions. The turbulence was so great that the heavy bombers were lifted and dropped hundreds of feet at a time. Two of the planes turned back and made it back to the airfield in Bermuda. The other five flew on, and were never seen again.

Tragic as it was, the loss of the five planes was seen as one of the hazards of wartime flying. The events that really put the Bermuda Triangle on the map happened almost exactly one year later, when the war was over.

Flight 19 was a routine training mission. On 5 December 1945, five US Navy Avenger bombers took off from their base in Fort Lauderdale, Florida. Each plane held a crew of three, pilot, radio operator and gunner. The Avengers were extremely powerful single-engine planes with a top speed of 300 miles an hour. They were combat-proved planes of the type which had sunk the Japanese super-battleship *Yamoto*. Fold-back wings enabled them to be used from land bases or from aircraft carriers. The aim of the current training mission was to perform bombing runs on some wrecks dotted along a sandbank off the island of Bimini. The flight leader was Lieutenant

Charles Taylor, an experienced pilot who had served in the war. Captain Stivers, another experienced officer, was piloting one of the planes.

The first part of the mission went exactly according to plan. The bombing runs were carried out satisfactorily and the little squadron turned homewards. Fifteen minutes before the planes were due to land back at Fort Lauderdale, the control tower operator heard Lieutenant Taylor's voice: "Calling tower. This is an emergency. We seem to be off course. We cannot see land."

The controller was amazed. It was a simple straightforward flight, weather conditions were reasonable and Lieutenant Taylor was an experienced pilot. Even if he had suffered a compass-failure, he should have been able to navigate by the sun. And what about the instruments on all the other planes? Had they all failed as well? The message came again: "We cannot see land. Repeat, we cannot see land." The controller kept his voice calm. "What is your position?" "We are not sure of our exact position. We cannot be sure just where we are. We seem to be lost."

The controller told Taylor to fly due west. If they were anywhere off the Florida coast, this would bring them back in sight of land.

There was panic in Taylor's voice. "We don't know which way is west." Chillingly, Taylor added, "Everything is wrong — strange. We cannot be sure of any direction. Even the ocean doesn't look the way it should."

As news of what was happening spread through the base, officers crowded into the control tower. Broken up by static, the voices of other pilots of Flight 19 crackled through the intercom. Everyone seemed to be in a state of total panic and confusion. Asked to estimate his position, Lieutenant Taylor said he thought they were somewhere off the Florida Keys — which meant that he was an incredible distance from his original flight path. At about 4 p.m. Lieutenant Taylor suddenly announced that he was handing over command to Captain Stivers.

Even the experienced Stivers seemed unable to sort things out. He sounded just as disorientated and confused as the other pilots. "We are not sure where we are," he reported. "We think we must be 225 miles south-east of base. We must have passed over Florida and be in the Gulf of Mexico."

There was more static and then his voice came again. "It looks like we're entering white water. . ." Another voice came through the crackling static. "We're completely lost." Those were the last words ever heard from Flight 19.

By now a rescue plane was already on its way – a Mariner flying boat, commanded by Lieutenant Cone. The Mariner was an enormous plane, with an 124-foot wing span. Her thirteen-man crew was trained in rescue operations and the flying boat was equipped with every kind of rescue equipment – including self-inflating life-rafts with built-in radio transmitters. The Mariner carried sufficient fuel to stay in the air for 24 hours.

Half an hour after the giant flying boat took off, its radio operator sent a message to the control tower. They were already approaching the last-known position of the missing flight. So far there was still no sign of the five Avengers.

Soon afterwards Lieutenant Cone sent back another position report, adding that he was encountering high winds. Then nothing. There was no distress call – but the giant flying boat was never heard of again. The Mariner had vanished – as completely and mysteriously as the missing flight of Avengers.

As soon as contact with the Mariner was lost, a fleet of Navy and coastguard vessels put to sea. 18 ships and 242 planes took part in the search.

Soon they were joined by the aircraft carrier *Solomons* and her 34 planes. But even with these reinforcements, nothing was found, not even any wreckage. After examining all the evidence the subsequent board of enquiry came up with no useful conclusions. One of its members said, "We're not even able to make a good *guess* as to what happened. They vanished as completely as if they'd flown to Mars."

The missing Avengers were found, however – but not until over forty-five years later. In May 1991 a team of divers, hunting for sunken Spanish treasure-ships, found the five Avengers ten miles off the Florida coast. They were on the bottom of the ocean in 750 feet of water, all in the same two mile area. No trace of the missing flying boat was found.

At last we know where the missing Avengers went down. But we still don't know why. Why were the two experienced pilots on the mission unable to bring the lost squadron back to base? Even if all their instruments had failed at once – which scarcely seems possible – all they had to do was fly with the afternoon sun on their left and they would have reached land. If they had encountered freak weather conditions, why didn't they mention them during the considerable time when the flight was in communication with the control tower?

There are still many questions to be answered. Why did *all* the pilots seem to be dazed and confused? What did Taylor mean by "Everything looks wrong – strange" ? Did some mysterious magnetic force strike Flight 19, confusing navigational instruments and pilots alike?

Since the disappearance of Flight 19, more planes and ships have gone missing, sometimes at the rate of one a month. Many of these later disappearances are almost as puzzling, though none have been on quite the same scale.

In 1947, the US Army Air Force lost a C-45 Superfortress, somewhere 100 miles off Florida. In 1948 a British airliner informed Bermuda it would arrive on schedule – and vanished with its 41 passengers. That same year a DC-3 with 32 passengers sent a message to Miami Airport. "We are approaching the field. All is well." The plane never arrived and was never seen again. In 1950 an American freighter vanished, in 1952 a British transport, in 1954 a US Navy Lockheed Constellation.

The list goes on and on continuing to the present day. Such explanations as UFO attack, and undersea alien bases have been freely suggested. Meanwhile, the mystery of the Bermuda Triangle is still unsolved. As the US Government admitted after an official enquiry: "Despite efforts by the United States Navy, Air Force and Coast Guard, no reasonable explanation to date has been found for the vanishments."

Tunguska — 1908

The Bermuda Triangle mystery stretches over hundreds of years – and thousands of miles of sea. The Tunguska Event occurred in one specific place and time. But exactly what occurred is still very much a mystery.

On the morning of 30 June 1908 a streak of fire shot down from the Siberian sky. When it reached the ground there was a vast cloud of black smoke followed by a shattering explosion. In a village hundreds of miles away, the ground shook, buildings trembled, and villagers fell on their knees, convinced that Judgement Day had arrived. A peasant resting on his porch felt a scorching blast of heat and saw a massive fireball in the sky. The blast from the subsequent explosion hurled him from his porch, knocking him uncon-

The Trans–Siberian–Railway

scious. A man ploughing the fields had his shirt burned from his back and received a painful burn down one side of his body. A train-driver on the Trans-Siberian railway halted his train because he thought something inside one of the goods-wagons he was pulling must have exploded.

The explosion, whatever it was, had happened in the remote Tunguska River valley, one of the most isolated parts of Siberia. The fireball devastated 80 square miles of countryside, destroying millions of trees. Whole herds

of reindeer were destroyed, and any survivors were badly blistered. The blast sent out seismic waves which travelled twice around the earth. The sound of the explosion was heard 500 miles away .

Because of the remoteness of the area, and the less advanced state of communications at the time, the world paid surprisingly little attention to what had happened. Freak weather conditions were recorded, and spectacularly colourful dawns and sunsets, caused by an unusual amount of dust in the air. It wasn't until after the First World War and the Russian revolution that anyone got round to making a proper investigation.

After the revolution, Lenin, leader of the newly Communist Russia was determined to show that Soviet science was the equal of any country in the world. For this reason he encouraged Russian scientists in their research. To this end, in 1927 Professor Leonid Kulik of the Soviet Academy of Science was commissioned to investigate the incident at Tunguska. Between 1927 and 1930 he led a number of expeditions to the Tunguska region. He found a ruined landscape dotted with craters, and mile upon mile of rotted tree-trunks. He spoke to witnesses of the blast, who told him of a fireball sweeping across the sky. Several of them swore it had changed direction before landing, heading first towards Lake Baikal and then swerving away. The smoke and the shattering explosion had been seen and heard by people who were anything from 50 to 250 miles away . . . Kulik also discovered that the explosion had had a strange effect on the trees and wildlife of the area. The trees that had survived were shooting up in strange shapes and at a rapid rate. Ants and insects were found in the Tunguska region which existed nowhere else. Kulik was completely baffled by this. To present-day scientists it suggests the kind of mutations caused by atomic radiation.

Kulik was convinced that the Tunguska explosion had been caused by a giant meteor striking Earth. Scientific knowledge at the time saw no other explanation. But several strange features of the explosion always puzzled him.

He was unable to find any remains at all of what must surely have been a meteorite of enormous size. There wasn't even any sign of a crater. Scientists who studied the results of the atomic bombs at Hiroshima and Nagasaki found no craters either. An atomic blast spreads sideways. An atomic blast also produces strange and lasting disturbances in the Earth's magnetic field. Even today such disturbances can be traced around Tunguska.

Various scientific explanations have been suggested, many of them highly imaginative. Some scientists think that the explosion was caused by a miniature black hole striking Earth. However, such a black hole would have gone straight through the Earth, and there are no records of it coming out on the other side.

Another suggestion is that Earth was hit by a chunk of anti-matter. Coming into contact with normal matter, i.e. the Earth, anti-matter would simply explode leaving only atomic radiation behind. It's a tempting theory, but since the very existence of anti-matter is theoretical, a theory it must remain.

Later Soviet scientists inclined to the theory

that the explosion was caused by a comet. This would account for the radiation, and for the enormous amounts of dust released into the atmosphere. However, it is rare for comets, especially large ones, to strike the Earth – or even to approach closely without being first detected and recorded. No such comet was recorded in 1908.

A Russian science-fiction writer called Alexander Kasantev has another explanation for the Tunguska explosion and its strange after-effects.

In his book, *Visitors from the Cosmos* he suggests that an alien space craft with an incredibly powerful atomic drive went out of control, overheating as it hit the Earth's atmosphere. It headed for Lake Baikal in a desperate attempt to make a "soft" landing and exploded before it could reach it.

Alexander Kasantev had visited Hiroshima and Nagasaki, and saw many significant similarities to the Tunguska site. It's interesting to note that he brought out his theory just *before* the UFO craze began in the USA.

Meteor, comet, black hole, or anti-matter?

We may never know. But something very strange happened at Tunguska in 1908, and struck the earth a shattering hammer-blow from out of nowhere. So keep watching the skies. After all, it could always happen again – maybe somewhere a lot more crowded than Tunguska . . .

CHAPTER 9
ECOLOGICAL HORRORS

The horrors that the Earth can inflict on us, are more than equalled by the horrors that, thanks to progress, we can now inflict upon the Earth – and on ourselves. Here are just a few of them.

Exxon Valdez – 1989

One of the great resources of Alaska is oil. Not the kind that runs cars and engines, but thick, black crude oil straight from the ground. Before the oil is of use to mankind it must be refined in refineries in Texas and in California. So the oil, millions of gallons of it, is taken from oil-well to refinery in giant vessels called supertankers, enormous ships with decks the size of four or five football pitches, highly computerized with relatively small crews. That's where the trouble sometimes starts.

The oil boom turned Valdez, Alaska into a boom town, one of the busiest supertanker ports in the world. Some tanker captains spend years on the Valdez–California–Valdez run alone. One of them was Captain Hazelwood, of the tanker *Exxon Valdez*.

On the evening of 3 March 1989, the *Exxon Valdez* left the port of Valdez and set sail for Long Beach, California. For the first two hours of the journey, the harbour pilot was responsible for the huge vessel's safety. After that, the responsibility returned to the captain. When the pilot had left the ship, Captain Hazelwood ordered a course change. He was worried about the amount of ice shown on the radar, so he called the port controller and asked permission to shift to the inbound sea lane, which was clearer. Since no inbound ships were expected, the controller gave his permission.

Captain Hazelwood's plan was to sail clear of the ice, and then to turn south-west. He would then take the giant ship through a narrow passage between the underwater rocks of Bligh Reef in Prince William Sound and one of the biggest ice floes. Most people would have considered this a pretty difficult piece of navigation, but Captain Hazelwood wasn't too worried. After all, he'd done this run many times before. Moreover, he had great confidence in all his officers.

Perhaps he was overconfident. Just before midnight, Captain Hazelwood ordered the ship's computer to start the build-up to full sea speed. Then he went below, leaving Third Mate Gregory Cousins, who was officer of the watch, in charge of the deck. Cousins had been ordered to make a right-hand turn after reaching a fixed navigational point. For some reason, he was about five minutes late making the turn. It might seem like a very small error. However, it meant that when the tanker actually did turn, she was a mile further ahead on her course than she ought to have been. Suddenly there came a terrible grinding sound. The ship had struck the underwater reef.

Third Mate Cousins called down to the captain, but it was too late. The damage was already done. Captain Hazelwood came on deck and took charge. His greatest worry was that the ship might slip from the reef and break her back. By varying the engine power, he kept the ship close to the reef in an attempt to minimize the damage. However, by now the ship was surrounded by a giant oil slick. There were long rents in the ship's hull under the water-line, and crude oil was flooding out into the sea. Captain Hazelwood reported the accident to the authorities on shore.

What followed proved that those authorities were quite unprepared to deal with an oil-spill of this size. It took the clean-up team ten hours to get to the site.

When they got there they had no booms — the one essential piece of equipment needed to contain an oil-spill. Detergents failed to work because the sea was too calm. Attempts to

The Exxon Valdez

burn off the oil proved an utter failure. The US Coastguard had a small fleet of damage-control vessels that might have been able to help. Unfortunately it was thousands of miles away, in San Francisco.

By the end of March, the oil slick had spread

over 900 miles of sea. It flooded into the hundreds of little rocky coves that lined Prince William Sound, coating the creatures that lived in them with thick, black, choking oil.

Despite the efforts by concerned people to clean the creatures up, the effect on the local wildlife was utterly devastating . It has been estimated that 86 000 birds, 1000 sea otters, 200 seals and 25 000 fish were killed by the oil.

In the weeks while the *Exxon Valdez* oil spill was slowly being dealt with, 10 000 000 gallons of crude oil flooded into the sea. The long-term damage to wild life and the environment is impossible to estimate. The oil remained to pollute the coves for a very long time, affecting future generations of wild life. Even when birds survive the effects of an oil slick, their health and their breeding cycle are affected for years to come.

Although Captain Hazelwood had done everything possible to save the situation after the catastrophe, he was still held largely responsible for letting it occur. He was particularly criticized for going below and leaving his Third Mate in charge of a difficult navigational manoeuvre. When tests proved that Captain Hazelwood had broken company regulations by drinking immediately before the ship sailed, his fate was sealed. He was dismissed from the company.

Because of the sheer scale of the oil spill, there was a storm of public protest. The Exxon Company was accused of a slow and inefficient response to the disaster, and its petrol stations were boycotted. The company president promised a billion dollars' worth of aid to help clean up the oil spill, and compensate fishermen ruined by the disaster.

After the accident, tanker companies tightened up their anti-drink regulations still further. New tankers were built with a double hull, in order to cut down the effects of any future accidents.

Exxon Valdez wasn't the first major oil spill to damage the environment. The *Amoco Cadiz* oil spill off France in 1971, and the spill caused by the collision of two ships in the Caribbean in 1979 caused even more damage. While supertankers continue to carry millions of tons of crude oil about the world, the *Exxon Valdez* disaster probably won't be the last . . .

Another ecological disaster, one that cost the lives of thousands of men women and children, occurred in central India in 1984.

Bhopal – 1984

One of the worst industrial accidents ever recorded took place at Bhopal in India on 3 December 1984. It was a direct result of bringing advanced technology to a Third World nation. With hindsight, of bringing too much, too soon.

There are big advantages to a western industrial nation in setting up some of its industries in the Third World. It can be seen as a benefactor bringing the benefits of progress to a backward country. It can also take advantage of inexpensive sites, lower building costs and, above all, cheap labour. The trouble is, much of the cheap labour will also be relatively unskilled. In Third World countries, there aren't the same laws to protect workers, so safety standards can slip. This can be dangerous enough in a car factory – in a place working with deadly chemicals, it can be catastrophic.

The Union Carbide Pesticide Plant was located in the poorest part of Bhopal, a small city in central India. Workers' huts were

crowded around the factory. The plant, which manufactured a pesticide called Sevin, had been closed down because of technical problems, and was just starting up again.

Sevin was made by mixing together three chemicals, carbon tetrachloride, alpha napthol and methyl isocyanate, known as MIC. There were problems with the giant mixing tanks, one of which was leaking nitrogen, and with keeping the MIC at the correct temperature.

The plant had been losing money recently and because of cost cutting, vital instruments had not been properly maintained. Number Six, one of the MIC tanks, was not being maintained at the proper temperature. It also had a faulty valve. As a result it was overfilled.

At this point mechanical and human errors started to pile up. A worker was ordered to clean a section of pipe that filtered MIC to the storage tanks. He connected a hose to the pipe and left it flowing. The supervisors knew that water reacted violently with MIC to create a poisonous gas, but the worker didn't know anything about a leaky valve. It wasn't his job. The water flowed from the hose for three hours.

Late that night it became obvious that pressure in the MIC tank was far too high. The duty supervisor saw the readings but he assumed that they must be wrong. Instruments often didn't work properly. Soon the eyes and noses of the workers on duty started to smart. But even this wasn't unusual. Minor gas leaks were quite common. By midnight the smell of gas was much worse and pressure in the MIC tank was rising alarmingly. The supervisor ordered all the water in the factory turned off. But it was already too late. Water was reacting with MIC and the deadly vapour was pouring out, blinding and choking workers.

The alarm went off at last and the fire brigade arrived. They attempted to place a wall of water round the escaping gas. But hose pressure only reached 100 feet, and the gas rose higher. A device called a gas scrubber was supposed to neutralize the escaping gas – but it wasn't working. Gas poured from the scrubber stack and drifted over the sleeping slums of Bhopal.

Inside the gas-filled factory, workers in oxygen masks struggled desperately to control the leak. The factory manager told a supervisor to turn on the flare tower and burn off the escaping gas. But the flare tower was out of service, waiting for a vital piece of pipe to arrive from America. The manager then told the supervisor to drain the MIC into an empty spare tank. All the spare tanks were already filled with MIC.

Gas poured out of the factory into the early hours of the morning. At 3 a.m. the factory manager sent a man to inform the police about the accident. Asked why he hadn't reported it earlier, he said it wasn't company policy to involve local authorities in gas leaks.

Meanwhile a deadly cloud of poison gas was drifting over Bhopal. Some people had heard the factory alarms going off. But then, the alarms were always going off. They didn't take it too seriously. Lots of people simply went back to sleep – and died while they were sleeping. Others woke up choking, dashed outside and breathed in more of the deadly fumes. Eyes streaming, choking and gasping for breath, people were dying all over Bhopal, in their houses and in the streets. Even the birds and insects were falling dead from out of the sky.

The panic spread swiftly. It was increased, if anything by the police, who toured the streets shouting, "Poison gas is escaping. Run! Run!" Everyone who could possibly manage tried to flee from the doomed city. Soon the roads were choked with fleeing refugees, many of them collapsing even as they tried to get away. A cloud of poisonous gas descended on Bhopal railway station, killing station workers, passengers and train staff all at once. Hospitals and medical services were totally overwhelmed. One hospital was recording a death a minute.

One mother later described how she woke up choking and vomiting and tried to carry her two small children to safety. Too weak to carry both she let one fall, and staggered on. The mother and remaining child survived, the one left behind died. Tragedies like this were repeated a thousand times.

By dawn the streets of Bhopal were filled with dead bodies. Over 2000 people died. Over 200 000 suffered after-effects that would last for years. Young children were hardest hit.

No one seemed to know what to do for the best, or even what the correct treatment should be. Union Carbide doctors said later that a wet cloth over the face would provide effective protection – but not enough people knew this at the time.

It took weeks to clear up the terrible effects of the tragedy. There were endless cremations. Bodies had to be buried in mass graves. The Indian Government sent in thousands of armed troops and police officers to run the refugee camps and maintain order.

A year after the accident, many of those injured were still suffering terrible after-effects. Some were blind. Others had trouble eating, sleeping and breathing. There was damage to the victims' kidneys, livers and stomachs.

When it was all over, attempts were made to fix the blame. When Union Carbide company officers arrived from America they were promptly arrested – but they were later released. The Indian Government decided to sue the company in the American Courts for compensation for the victims. The case dragged on for years. The tragedy seems to have been caused by a combination of factors. First, the out-dated, badly maintained equipment that failed in a real emergency. Secondly, the insufficiently trained staff and poor communication between workers and management, so that one mistake combined with another to terrible effect. And, finally, Union Carbide's decision to site a technologically complex, and potentially dangerous, chemical project in a little Indian town – without providing the maintenance and back-up needed to make it safe.

There is one kind of disaster more dreaded than any other – not only because of the terrible devastation it can cause, but because of the incalculably long-term nature of its effects.

Ever since the discovery of atomic power, the invention and use of the atomic bomb, and the subsequent development of atomic energy for peaceful use, we have lived in dread of a major nuclear accident. Anti-nuclear campaigners warned of the possibility of the "China Syndrome" – an atomic explosion followed by a "meltdown" so powerful that it would burn its way right through the planet, all the way to China.

That hasn't happened – yet. But some very frightening nuclear accidents have already occurred. Their effects are still very much with us today.

Windscale – 1957

On the afternoon of 10 October 1957, the number-one uranium pile at Windscale (now called Sellafield) plutonium factory in Cumbria, England, started to overheat. The pile rapidly became red hot, releasing radioactive iodine particles into the air. When the fire was discovered, workers in protective clothing tried to put it out with carbon dioxide. It didn't work.

It was decided to treat the fire like any other, and call the fire brigade. On the morning of the 11 October, plant officials and local firefighters took a hose to the top of the containment dome around the pile and poured water on to the fire. Since there had never really been a nuclear fire of this kind before, nobody quite knew what would happen. The rest of the plant workers and officials took cover at what they hoped would be a safe distance.

Fortunately the water put out the fire, although it also released radioactive steam into the atmosphere. Nevertheless there was a general feeling of relief. There had been no explosion and the dreaded meltdown hadn't happened. But there *were* long-term consequences. Large amounts of radioactive iodine-131 had been released into the atmosphere. Local farmers were told that the milk from their cows would be radioactive. A ban was put on all milk for 200 miles around. 30 000 gallons of it had to be dumped. Hundreds of cows and sheep were slaughtered and burned. Even then it wasn't over, though the really serious consequences took some time to show themselves. As time went by the number of deaths from cancer rose significantly amongst those who had been exposed to radiation. So far over thirty deaths have been linked to the accident.

Three Mile Island — 1979

In 1979 there was a nuclear accident at the Three Mile Island nuclear power plant. The plant was located on an island in the Susquehanna River, near Harrisburg, Pennsylvania. Because of a combination of design faults and human error, the reactor over-heated, melting several hundred of its fuel rods, and radioactive steam was released into the atmosphere.

As with Windscale there was no explosion, and no immediate deaths from the accident. But there was a marked rise in deaths, particularly infant deaths, in the years that followed.

Chernobyl — 1986

With Windscale, and with Three Mile island, one gets the feeling of a lucky escape. The feared catastrophe had somehow failed to materialize. The worst hadn't happened.

At Chernobyl, it did.

Chernobyl nuclear power plant is in Pripayat, in what was then the USSR, 70 miles from Kiev, capital of the Ukraine. It is one of the largest, and one of the oldest, of Russia's nuclear power plants.

Pripayat is, or rather was, a quiet country town in the Ukraine. Lots of trees grew in the streets and public gardens. Storks nested on the flat roofs of the houses. Before the Chernobyl nuclear power plant was built, Pripayat was something of a holiday resort. There was fishing and swimming in the river and the local lakes. Today Pripayat is a ghost town, an area of contaminated desolation. No one will ever live or work there again.

The appalling irony of this worst of all nuclear disasters is that it was caused by a series of efficiency tests. The purpose of the tests was to see how long the turbine and generator, powered by the reactor, would go on running if the reactor failed and power was reduced to nothing.

The scientists carrying out the tests had one main problem. There was a likelihood that the reduction of the power would trigger the reactor's safety mechanisms, shutting it down completely all at once – which would spoil the test. With what seems like incredible folly – and in defiance of all safety regulations – the scientists decided that there was a simple answer. They would disconnect all the reactor's emergency safety systems before beginning the test.

On the afternoon of 25 April they shut down the safety systems and started the tests. Power from the reactor was gradually reduced to a fraction of its normal capacity. The scientists proceeded with their tests, noting the effects of the shutdown on the generator and turbine. One of them noticed a computer printout warning that the reactor was starting to overheat. He decided it wasn't significant and ignored it.

By the morning of 26 April the reactor had overheated to a point where the safety systems would automatically have closed it down – if they had been operational. But they weren't. Just under two hours later, the reactor blew up. All the technicians close to the reactor were killed immediately. Three separate explosions, one after the other, sent its 1000-ton steel roof flying into the air. An enormous fireball shot up into the sky, and 1000-foot flames roared up after it. The burning reactor was visible for miles around.

Emergency teams in protective clothing attempted to pull the dead and dying away from the reactor. Firemen tried vainly to put out the roaring blaze. Temperatures had risen so incredibly high that the floors were melting under their feet. By now the burning reactor was pouring a stream of red-hot radioactive material into the atmosphere. Realizing the danger, the authorities ordered a complete evacuation of the nearby town of Pripayat. The other reactors at Chernobyl were all shut down. Military units arrived to supervise the evacuation, and all roads in and out of the town were blocked. A fleet of 11 000 buses was organized to ferry out the town's inhabitants, who were ordered to bring only a minimum of luggage. A total of 20 000 people were evacuated from Pripayat, and another 26 000 from the surrounding countryside.

Meanwhile the burning reactor continued to blaze unchecked. Some of the Russian technicians reacted like heroes, staying at their posts even when ordered to leave. Others,

perhaps understandably, fled in panic.

Meanwhile the senior scientists now in charge struggled desperately to find a way of quenching the blaze. They considered simply using water, as had been done at Windscale. But this fire was far bigger and it was burning "like a charcoal fire', as one witness said, at a temperature of 2500°C. Besides, too little water would be far worse than none at all. It might react with the red-hot graphite to form hydrogen. This could set off a major explosion, destroy more reactors and release even more radioactivity into the atmosphere. There was just no way of getting the truly colossal amount of water that would be needed to the site.

Some unknown Soviet genius came up with a novel solution. They would use helicopters to "bomb" the blaze with dampening materials that would absorb radiation and put out the fire as well. It was decided to use a mixture of sand, clay, lead, dolomite and boron, packed into sandbags.

Air Force Major-General Antoshkin was put in charge of the project. His helicopter pilots faced an incredibly hazardous operation, fully as dangerous as any wartime mission. They had to fly into a radioactive cloud, deliver their bombs on to an incredibly small target obscured by smoke and flame, and leave quickly before they absorbed dangerous amounts of radiation.

Considering that nothing like this had ever been done before, the pilots carried out their mission with extraordinary skill and determination. Ninety-three trips were made on the first day. By the second the number had risen to over 180. At first the pilots had to shove single sacks through the helicopter doors by hand. As the mission got under way, a quick-release tackle was improvised, so that six or eight sacks could be dropped at a time. No one really knew how much radiation the pilots were absorbing, or how badly it might affect them. The first wave of pilots flew completely unprotected. Later, lead shields were used in an attempt to give them some protection. The dangerous helicopter flights went on day after day, dumping sack after sack into the nuclear inferno.

What of the rest of the world while all this was going on? Authorities everywhere have a tendency to play down disasters of this kind. Authoritarian regimes, like the Soviet Union of the time, are even more likely to do so. But the scale of the nuclear disaster was so great that it couldn't possibly be concealed.

One morning after the Chernobyl fire, a worker at a Swedish nuclear plant turned up for work. Following the usual routine, he passed through the radiation detector – and set off an alarm. At first the safety inspector suspected a leak in his own factory – but the worker had just come in from outside. All the factory's newly arrived workers were tested – and all found positive. The dust on their clothes and shoes was radioactive.

Already scientific monitoring instruments in Sweden were picking up abnormal amounts of radioactivity in the atmosphere. Sweden reminded Russia that, according to international agreements, every country was required to inform its neighbours of any nuclear accident that might endanger them. The Soviet authorities issued a brief statement to the effect that an accident had occurred at Chernobyl, one of the reactors was damaged, and all appropriate measures were being taken. There were only 2 dead, and under 200 injured.

Inevitably the truth was starting to leak out. Radio hams – amateur radio operators – were picking up transmissions from Russia. A Dutch ham overheard a conversation between a Russian and a Japanese operator. The Russian spoke of hundreds of deaths and a reactor destroyed by meltdown.

An Israeli operator claimed to have spoken to people who actually lived near Chernobyl. They too had told him of an exploding reactor. The radioactive cloud spread over Poland, Hungary and Czechoslovakia. Finland and Denmark, as well as Sweden detected increased radioactivity.

Four days after the accident, the Soviet ambassador in Germany visited the German Foreign Ministry in Bonn. Did anyone in Germany know how to extinguish a graphite reactor fire? The question was passed on to the German Atomic Forum. But no one could help. Until then, nobody had believed that the graphite core of a reactor *could* catch fire.

The Russian Ambassador admitted that there had been a nuclear accident, and that radioactivity had been released near Chernobyl. He said the area had been evacuated, and the situation was now "under control".

The alarmed German government closed swimming pools and set up radioactivity checks on milk and fresh vegetables. As the news spread similar precaution were being taken in Holland, Italy and Switzerland. All over Europe, alarm, and anti-nuclear protest was growing. In response, increasingly worried governments were issuing reassuring statements – based more on hope than on scientific evidence.

The Chernobyl radioactive cloud reached Britain about a week after the accident. Here too the government made reassuring noises, saying the cloud would "clip the corner of Kent and then pass over the eastern part of East Anglia before being blown northwards out over the North Sea." There was no risk to the public. It was true that by the time the cloud reached Britain it was very much weakened. But it became obvious that the government had little idea of the real extent of the danger, and no real plans for dealing with nuclear disaster if it ever happened here.

On 13 May Yevgeny Velikov, one of Russia's leading scientists, told a press conference in Vienna that the reactor had stopped releasing fission products into the atmosphere. It had taken fourteen days and required the services of a large fleet of helicopters. The scientists working at the Chernobyl site knew that the danger wasn't over. There was still the possibility that the blocked-off reactor would overheat to meltdown-point, causing the dreaded "China Syndrome". Another possible danger was that the red-hot material from the reactor core might come into contact with the pool of water beneath the core, leading to yet another explosion.

The pool of water, part of the reactor's normal safety-system, could only be released by opening two control valves. But the control valves could only be reached by a journey through dark and narrow underground tunnels, now completely flooded by radioactive water. An engineer called Alexei Ananenko was one of the few people who knew exactly where the valves were. Bravely, he volunteered to go and open them. Another engineer called Valeri Bezpalov went with him to help. A third man, Boris Baranov held the underwater torch.

Protected by diving suits, all three made the terrifying journey. Before they reached the valves the lamp went out, leaving them in the total darkness of the flooded tunnels. They made the rest of the journey by feeling their way along the pipes. At last they reached the first valve. "We tried to turn it – it moved," said Ananenko later. "Our hearts pounded with joy but we couldn't say anything – we were wearing respirators. I showed Valeri the other valve. It budged too. A few minutes later the characteristic noise or splashing sound was heard. The water was going . . ."

The Russian engineers' final task was to build a thick cushion of concrete below the reactor. The soggy ground had to be frozen with liquid nitrogen before the necessary tunnels could be drilled. As an extra precaution, Russian soldiers, just back from the war in Afghanistan, were given the job of building a massive dyke, to prevent the radioactive water from draining into the Pripayat river. Once the base was in place, the reactor was completely encased in concrete, sealed into a tomb for the hundreds of years it will take for the radioactivity to fall to safe levels.

As soon as news of the disaster had spread, a Californian doctor called Robert Gale offered his help. Dr Gale was a world expert on bone-marrow transplants, a vital technique in the treatment of radiation victims. With the help of finance provided by millionaire Arnold Hammer, a team of international experts was flown to Russia together with thousands of dollars' worth of equipment. The team treated firefighters, scientists and technicians, and doctors who had been close to the scene of the accident, or who had come to help.

The patients were badly burned and hairless, racked with radiation sickness. Despite all the best efforts of the medical team, only a few of them survived. Dr Gale said later that the Chernobyl incident proved that medical science could do comparatively little to help the worst victims of a single nuclear disaster.

In the event of a really major catastrophe –
such as a nuclear war – nothing really effective could be done at all.

Official figures are hard to
come by, but it's reckoned that
over 30 people died as a direct
result of the accident.
However, it is estimated that
the death toll from cancers
caused by radiation, in
Russia and all over the
world, will run into
thousands. Today, ten
years later, children
around Pripayat are
suffering exceptional-
ly high rates of thy-
roid cancer. A similar
effect has been report-
ed very recently on the
Scottish island of
Benbecula.

The deadly effects of
Chernobyl are still being
monitored all over
the world. In
April 1996,
on the
tenth

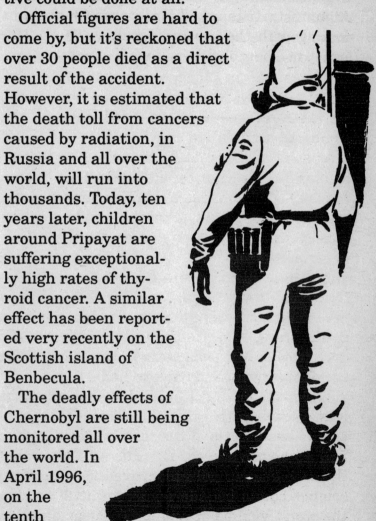

anniversary of the disaster, a conference was held in Vienna, sponsored by the World Health Organization. At the conference, Russian atomic scientists asked for international aid in dealing with the continuing after-effects. The legacy of Chernobyl is still with us today.

CHAPTER 10

SOME ASSORTED DISASTERS

Finally, here's an assorted collection of horribly unexpected events – just to show how suddenly disaster can strike. . .

Airships Ablaze

If ever there was an idea ahead of its time it was the airship. Huge, graceful, engine-powered balloons, carrying passengers and cargo in great gondola-like cabins suspended below, the great silver cigar-shaped airships were an astonishingly beautiful sight as they drifted through the skies.

Unfortunately they proved to be extremely unsafe – largely because their balloon-sections were usually filled with highly explosive hydrogen. Towards the end of the time when airships were in common use, it was already becoming possible to use the much safer helium gas.

Despite this advance in safety, some serious disasters put the airship out of favour, leading to its replacement by the less-graceful but more efficient aeroplane.

Here are two of the reasons why we don't see many airships these days.

The R101

The *R101* was the dream of just one man – Lord Cardington. He was Minister for Air in England back in 1930, when the *R101* set off on its last voyage. 200 yards long, and filled with 5 000 000 cubic feet of hydrogen, the giant airship was the largest flying machine in the world. The *R101* was Lord Cardington's particular pride and joy. He had even taken his title from the nationalized aircraft factory at Cardington in Bedfordshire, where the *R101* had been built. A firm believer in the future of airship travel, and anxious for England to lead the way in its development, Lord Cardington had become obsessed with his pet project, pushing the airship's construction ahead at full speed.

In the opinion of some of the engineers working on the project it had been pushed ahead rather too fast. When the airship was put into reverse the propellers broke off. A special rear engine had to be fitted so that the airship could manoeuvre. The separate gasbags inside the outer hull tended to move about, unbalancing the airship, so that it lurched and reeled at its mooring mast. In addition to all this, the hull suffered from frequent splits, some as long as 50 feet long. As a result of these rents, the entire hull was soon covered with patches. To cure this fault, the airship was cut in half, and an extra gas-bag inserted. Soon after this process was complete a 90 foot gash appeared in the side. This too had to be patched up.

In June 1930 the repaired and refurbished airship made an appearance at the Hendon Air Display. Unfortunately, the display didn't go quite according to plan. The airship began twisting and turning in the air before nose-diving towards the crowd, pulling out just 500 feet above the ground. The crowd applauded wildly, not realizing that the terrified pilot was desperately trying to get the airship back under control. He finally managed to get the airship down – hydrogen pouring from numerous leaks.

With a history like this, you might have expected the *R101* to have remained in the testing stage for a very long time. Not a bit of it, for Lord Cardington wouldn't hear a word against it. Despite his obsession with the success of the *R101* Lord Cardington had ambitions above the Air Ministry: he wanted to be Viceroy of India. (At the time, India was still part of the British Empire.) What would impress his future subjects more, he reasoned, than for him actually to arrive in the magnificent airship that he had inspired?

Therefore Lord Cardington announced his

intention of using the *R101* for a flight to India. Everyone involved in the project was horrified.

Designers, engineers, Air Ministry Inspectors, all insisted the the *R101* simply wasn't ready for such a long and dangerous voyage. Yet Lord Cardington refused to listen. "I must insist on the programme for the India flight being adhered to," he announced. "I have made my plans accordingly." He also issued a statement saying, "The *R101* is as safe as a house, at least to the millionth chance."

Subsequent events failed to justify Lord Cardington's lunatic optimism. Moreover, his folly was to cause the loss of a number of lives.

On the evening of 4 October 1930, the *R101* set off for India. The first part of the flight was across the English Channel and then on over France. It was a filthy night for air travel, with rain pouring down. The *R101* had never been tested in bad weather. The water on the hull weighed the airship down and over the channel it dipped dangerously low, before the pilot managed to restore height.

Observers saw the *R101* flying low over the French coast. Later estimates put her height at 300 feet. Then she was seen passing over the town of Beauvais as low as 200 feet. Suddenly watchers saw the nose of the airship dip – the hull had split near the nose and hydrogen was pouring out. As the airship dropped, crewmen struggled to bring her down safely. To an extent they succeeded. The *R101* made a relatively soft landing in a field, and one or two people managed to jump from the gondola beneath to the ground below. Most were not so lucky. There was a hiss of escaping hydrogen, and a sudden flash. There were two more explosions and the *R101* became a blazing inferno. Fifty-four passengers had boarded the *R101* when she set off for India.

Only six of them survived.

Lord Cardington, the man whose obstinate folly had done so much to bring about the disaster, was among the dead.

The Hindenburg

The fate of the *R101* did a lot to discourage airship development, but it didn't put an end to it. It took a second disaster to do that. The *Hindenburg* was Nazi Germany's pride and joy, after all, it was Germany's Graf von Zeppelin who had pioneered the development of the airship, and its use as a weapon in the First World War. Now Adolf Hitler was determined to follow the same glorious path. Built in 1935, named after one of Germany's First World War generals, the *Hindenburg* was intended to demonstrate the industrial power and the scientific superiority of Nazi Germany to an awe-struck world. And this giant airship was certainly an impressive sight, being 830 feet long and 125 feet high.

Germany could boast of never having had an airship disaster, and on the *Hindenburg*, safety standards were paramount. The crew wore asbestos suits and rope-soled slippers, so as to run no risk of igniting the hydrogen gas that filled the ship. All passengers had to hand in matches, lighters and all smoking materials before embarking. Those who wanted to smoke could only do so in a special pressurized lounge. Even then, the lighting of cigars or cigarettes was carried out for them by stewards in a second, even more secure, cabin.

The *Hindenburg* was a sort of luxury liner of the skies. Staterooms and lounges were furnished to the highest standards, and the finest food and wines were served. Passengers slept in comfort, in proper beds.

The *Hindenburg* was built and thoroughly tested in 1935. In 1936 she went into service on the America run, crossing from Frankfurt, Germany to New Jersey in America.

For over a year, the *Hindenburg* made crossing after crossing, surviving the worst of weather with no safety problems at all. But this record was not to last.

On 6 May 1937, the *Hindenburg* was approaching her landing point at Lakehurst, New Jersey. On the ground a radio reporter was waiting to describe her landing and it is thanks to him we have a firsthand account of this terrible disaster. Because of bad weather over the Atlantic, the airship had arrived ten hours late. The ship's commander delayed the actual landing for several hours for the same reason. At last the great cigar-shaped airship started drifting down. The reporter gives his account of the landing routine: "The ropes have been dropped, and they have been taken hold of by a number of men in the field. The back motors of the ship are holding it just enough to keep it . . ."

Suddenly his voice changes. "It's burst into flame! This is terrible . . . The flames are 500 feet in the sky. It's in smoke and flames now . . . those passengers . . ."

At this point the reporter's voice breaks. 'I'm going to have to step inside where I can't see it. I . . . I . . . folks, I'm going to have to stop for a while. This is the worst thing I've ever witnessed. It is one of the worst catastrophes in the world."

At the moment the guide ropes had been lowered for landing, the *Hindenburg* burst into flame. In thirty seconds the entire *Hindenburg* was ablaze. Passengers and crew could be seen jumping from the burning airship.

Fifteen passengers and

twenty crewmen died in the flames. Amazingly, sixty-two of the passengers and crew survived. Amongst them was Ernst Lehmann, the airship's first commander, who was travelling as an observer. He was found, badly hurt, in the charred remains of the airship, muttering, "I can't understand it . . ."

Lehmann lived for two more days. Asked on his deathbed what had caused the explosion he whispered, "Lightning . . ." But he still sounded uncertain. The official enquiry concluded that the explosion had been caused by "a freak electrical discharge in the atmosphere".

Another way of saying that they didn't know either.

The Nazis, paranoid as ever, muttered darkly about sabotage, and the Gestapo searched frantically for proof that the enemies of the Third Reich were involved. In this case they may just possibly have been right. The German Ambassador in Washington had received a letter warning him that there was a bomb on board the airship.

There is a theory that there was indeed a bomb, placed by an anti-Nazi crew member. The bomb was intended to go off after landing – but the *Hindenburg* landed ten hours late because of bad weather in the Atlantic and the saboteur failed to survive his own bomb.

Something else that failed to survive was the idea of the airship as a safe means of transport. The fate of the *Hindenburg* was one disaster too many.

Soon the great silver ships vanished from the skies . . .

Aberfan — 1966

Aberfan was a small mining village in the Welsh valleys. It was dominated by a sort of artificial mountain, a giant pile of slag known officially as Tip Number Seven. Today most of the mines are closed and many of the slag-heaps converted into green hills, but in the sixties the great black shapes loomed over many a mining village. Ugly as they were the slag-heaps were taken for granted, just a part of life.

It was raining on 21 October just as it had been raining for day after day. The rain turned the giant tip into a sort of wet and soggy slurry. Slowly and silently it began to move . . .

What made the resulting tragedy so unbearable was that the village's little primary school stood in the path of the moving black sludge.

Just after 9 a.m., a great mass of slurry

crashed into the school and the cottages that stood alongside. The silence was broken by a terrible grinding noise as the building was shattered, and by the shouts and screams of all those trapped inside.

Those in the part of the school facing the slag heap were overwhelmed at once. Teachers and children on the other side of the building got a little warning, and some of them were able to escape.

Eight-year-old Pat Lewis watched in amazement as the classroom wall started splitting open behind her teacher. She screamed and the teacher was able to get most of the class to safety. Pat's elder sister Sharon was one of those who didn't get away.

Pat herself ran home to her mother. Mrs Lewis, a trained nurse, ran back to the school. She climbed in through a broken window and saw about twenty children who had been swept to the top of the heap of slurry. She started helping them out.

Despite losing one of her own children, Mrs lewis turned a surviving classroom into a first-aid station, and worked all day helping the survivors. "No one came out alive after 11 a.m.," she said later.

One lucky little boy had been sent outside the school on an errand. He was lifted on top

of the great black slimy mass and carried along. He was buried on top of the pile and remembers men digging him out and muddy water pouring all over him. He lost three fingers and an ear and suffered massive internal injuries, but he survived. Another child had left the classroom to take her dinner money to the school secretary's office. She was trapped in the school corridor in mud and broken masonry, but she too survived.

As the news of the terrible catastrophe spread, everyone in Aberfan came to help. Police, firefighters and ambulance workers had scores of helpers – amongst them the miners themselves, many of whom had children trapped in the building. The rescue teams worked all day and all night too, by artificial lights. By next day it was clear that little more could be done.

That day 144 people died in Aberfan; 116 of them were children.

There was, of course, an official enquiry. It took six months and saw hundreds of witnesses. All that emerged was what everyone already knew – the tragedy should never have happened. It seemed the National Coal Board had no clear safety policy for dealing with slag heaps. Although mining engineers had warned for years that the Aberfan tip was unstable, no one took any notice and nothing was done. After the tragedy new safety regulations were put in place and rigidly enforced. But it was all too late for the children and parents of Aberfan.

Soccer Tragedies

When football commentators talk about tragedy, they usually mean the fumbled pass or the missed save that loses the match. But soccer has had its share of real tragedies as well.

Bradford – 1985

Bradford was an old stadium, built mostly of wood. Underneath the wooden seats, piles of rubbish had accumulated over the years and had never been cleared away.

That Saturday afternoon in 1985 the home team was up for promotion, and the crowd was bigger than usual. Just before half-time, someone dropped a match, or perhaps a cigarette end, through the gap in the floor under his seat and on to the rubbish below. The rubbish started to smoulder. Suddenly a whole section of seating seemed to explode into flame. The flames shot upwards, and instantly the roof was alight. The flames spread rapidly throughout the whole of the stadium. People looked for fire extinguishers, but there weren't any around. They'd been removed so football thugs couldn't use them as weapons. There weren't any emergency exits either. They'd been barred to keep gatecrashers out. Now they were keeping fire victims in.

Chunks of blazing tarpaulin dropped from the roof, wrapping up screaming fans in a blanket of fire. The Bradford fire caused the deaths of 56 people; two of them were children.

Heysel – 1985

The next tragedy happened only a few weeks later. This time it took place abroad – in Brussels' Heysel Stadium, where Liverpool United were playing the crack Italian team Juventus.

It was the European Cup final, and it was accompanied by all the usual international tensions. Rival fans fought running battles in the streets, while exasperated Belgian police struggled to keep them apart.

The police made a serious mistake at the very beginning of the game. They put a crowd of Italian fans in the end of the ground meant for Liverpool supporters. This time the trouble started even before the match. Some Liverpool supporters broke out of their own area and started pelting the Italians with bricks, lumps of metal, and anything else they could find.

The trapped Italian fans pressed against a concrete wall at the bottom of the stand. Under the pressure, the wall gave way. Like

water bursting a dam, crowds of enraged supporters flooded over the broken wall and on to
the pitch.

After that it was sheer mayhem. Angry
groups of rival fans were fighting all over
the pitch. The Belgian police, like most
Continental police forces, are not known for
the gentle touch. They charged the crowd,
swinging batons and cracking heads indiscriminately. Badly-needed medical help took
hours to arrive. By the time it was all
over, there were 39 dead, 6 of them British,
33 Italian. British fans were banned from
Continental matches.

Air Crash on the Ground

Whatever the statistics, quite a few people feel
that flying is dangerous. They feel there's something unnatural about being trapped inside tons
of metal hurtling through the air.

But one of the worst air crashes of all time
took place on the ground . . .

A sort of side-effect of terrorism caused the
Tenerife air crash. On 27 March 1977, a bomb
exploded harmlessly in a shop in Las Palmas
airport on the neighbouring island of Gran
Canaria.

There was a threat of a second bomb and because of this threat — which proved to be groundless — all aircraft heading for Gran Canaria were diverted to the already crowded airport on the holiday island of Tenerife.

Things were made worse by the foggy weather. The diverted planes included two Boeing 707s. Both had originally been heading for Las Palmas. One was a KLM flight from Amsterdam, the other a Pan American Airways flight from New York. Now, because of the diversion, both planes were sitting on the fog-bound runway in Tenerife. Late in the afternoon, the pilots of both planes were pleased to hear that Las Palmas airport was once again clear for landing. Because of the fog, visibility was very bad, so following the instructions of the control tower, both pilots taxied cautiously towards the take-off point at the end of the main runway. The KLM pilot was told to taxi to the end of the runway and then backtrack. He did so and reported, "KLM ready for take-off." The Pan Am pilot was told to taxi up behind the KLM plane, but to turn off on the left, leaving the runway clear for the KLM flight.

Then the control tower asked the Pan Am pilot if the turn was complete. He replied, "Not yet." "Complete the turn and advise when runway is clear," ordered the controller. Perhaps the KLM pilot overheard only the last few words – and thought the message was meant for him. Whatever the reason he radioed information about his projected flight plan after take-off to the tower. The end of the message, which was indistinct, was, "KLM now ready on take-off."

But the Pan Am plane was still blocking the runway.

Suddenly the Pan Am pilot saw the massive KLM jet taxiing straight towards him out of the fog.

"Look at him!" he shouted. "The sonofabitch is coming!

'Get off! Get off!'" yelled the Pan Am co-pilot.

By now the KLM pilot could see the other plane. But he was moving too fast to stop in time. In a last desperate gamble he tried to raise his aircraft, to hop over the one in front. But he was too late. The nose of the KLM plane lifted – and then its body slammed into the Pan Am jet, cutting it in half. The Pan Am plane burst into flames.

Both aircraft were crowded with holiday passengers, and the result was total catastrophe. Some passengers were thrown from the wrecked and burning Pan American plane and made their way to safety, many more burned to death, trapped in their seats.

The KLM plane slammed back down on the runway, spun round in a circle and then exploded into flame. All 248 people on board were killed immediately.

There were 396 people on board the Pan American plane. Only 70 survived the crash, and 9 of those died later in hospital. In total, 583 people lost their lives, in one of the worst disasters in airline history. All because of a harmless bomb in an airport shop and the false alarm that followed.

Disasters in Space

Considering the appalling dangers and the almost totally unknown risks of space travel, the number of space-disasters is astonishingly low. But, inevitably, there have been some. One came at the very beginning of the space race.

America's first casualty was really a victim of the space race – the intense rivalry between America and Russia. Russian rockets used an oxygen-nitrogen atmosphere, like air itself, in their spacecraft. The Americans, whose rockets were initially less powerful, saved weight by using oxygen alone. But if American spacecraft were lighter, the volatile nature of oxygen made them less safe.

On 7 January 1967, astronauts Gus Grissom, Roger Chaffee and Ed White reported for duty at Cape Canaveral. They were there simply to practise cockpit drill. This involved lying on their backs in the command capsule wearing their spacesuits, obeying various technical instructions, and transmitting test readings from their instruments to the technicians in ground control. It was a routine which they had carried out time and again. Suddenly one of the ground control technicians saw his screen go dark. As he tried to adjust it he heard a voice shout, "Fire! I smell fire!" There were a few seconds silence and then Ed White's voice. "Fire in the cockpit!"

They heard the trapped astronauts pounding desperately on the door of the capsule.

Seconds later they heard Roger Chaffee's voice. "We're on fire. Get us outa here." Then silence.

The rescue team raced to the top of the launch tower. They opened the red-hot doors of the escape hatch and flames roared out of the capsule. At this point the launch director ordered the rescue team to move back.

It was too late to do anything for the men in the capsule; they were already dead.

The rescue team had to wait for another six

hours before the launch director judged that the capsule could be opened without risk of an explosion. During all this time the bodies of the three dead astronauts were clearly visible on the control room monitors. At midnight, the three dead bodies were carried out of the burned-out cockpit.

Later investigation uncovered the probable cause of the disaster. A loose wire in the control panel had caused a spark which, in the pure oxygen atmosphere, had caused a fire. If the Americans had been using an oxygen/nitrogen atmosphere, like the Russians, the fire might never have started.

Despite this tragedy, NASA decided they were too far down the road to change the atmosphere now. They designed some new spark-proof electrical circuitry and went ahead. This time it worked. On 21 July 1969, *Apollo 11* put Neil Armstrong on the moon. America had won the space race – at the cost of three lives.

Salyut One

The Russians too paid a price for their success in space. Beaten in the moon-landing race, they decided to forge ahead in another area – the space station. On 6 June 1971 they put the world's first space station, *Salyut One*, into orbit.

On the same day, three cosmonauts from the *Soyuz 11* docked with the space station and went inside.

After spending a record twenty-three days in the space station, the three cosmonauts, Dobrovolsky, Patsayev, and Volkov set off to return to Earth. Their orders were to remain in the capsule on landing, in case their time in space had weakened their muscles. A medical team would carry them out. "Don't worry," said Dobrovolsky cheerfully, on receiving the instruction. "We'll sit back and let you do all the work!"

Releasing its parachutes, the capsule floated gently back to earth in a perfect landing. As always, radio contact had been lost in the last stages of the descent.

It hadn't been picked up again yet, but no one was too worried. After all, the cosmonauts were safely down. At last the recovery team secured the capsule. Eager to greet their returned comrades, the medical team opened it up. To their horror, they discovered that all three Soviet cosmonauts were dead. The explosive charges used to detach the capsule from the space lab had blown open a valve in the capsule's hatch. The space capsule had been gradually leaking air all the way back to Earth. What Soviet ground control had landed was not a capsule but a coffin.

Challenger - 1986

The most shocking space disaster of all began as the latest of a series of missions that had become almost routine. Perhaps a dangerous complacency had set in.

The *Challenger* space shuttle had already flown 24 successful missions. The shuttle represented the new face of space technology, dedicated to peaceful scientific uses. Its latest mission had something special about it. It was the first to take an ordinary civilian into space. The civilian, schoolteacher Christa McAuliffe, had been chosen from thousands of applicants.

Her part in the mission was to teach two fifteen-minute lessons from the space shuttle as it orbited the Earth. Her words would be transmitted by closed-circuit television to children all over America. However, as Christa prepared for the trip of a lifetime, she was unaware that a safety debate about the shuttle had been raging behind the scenes. Because temperatures at Cape Canaveral had been abnormally low recently, scientists were concerned that ice forming on the hull might break off during the launch and damage the shuttle's heat-resistant tiles. An even more serious worry concerned the rubber "O-rings" that sealed joints in the capsule's boosters. Engineers from the firm that made the booster rockets were concerned that the abnormally cold weather might make the O-rings brittle,

and less well-fitting – allowing dangerous gases to escape. The rocket engineers were convinced that the launch ought to be postponed.

NASA was firmly against it. There had been two bad-weather postponements already. On the second, the forecast had been wrong and the actual weather on the day had turned out to be perfect for a space-launch. NASA had been made to look foolish.

It's possible that the presence of Christa McAuliffe had something to do with NASA's insistence on going ahead. The idea of taking a schoolteacher into space had come from President Ronald Reagan himself. It was a public relations gesture, a way to show that space was for everyone. There had been a certain amount of criticism recently about the billions of dollars spent on the space race. Now that the excitement of the moon landings was past, the American public was losing interest, beginning to wonder if the space programme was really giving value for money. President Reagan, who was by now committed to his "Star Wars" defence programme, was keen for a successful space launch to go ahead. Whatever the reason, the rocket engineers were overruled, their worries ignored.

On the morning of 28 January 1986 the

seven astronauts, including schoolteacher Christa McAuliffe, made their way on board the space shuttle, watched by an enthusiastic crowd.

Commander Dick Scobee and pilot Michael Smith took their places on the flight deck. Electrical engineer Judith Resnick and physicist Ronald McNair sat directly behind them. Christa McAuliffe, aerospace expert Ellison Onizuka and engineer Greg Jarvis occupied places on the mid-deck. The instrument checks were completed and the countdown began.

The crowds gathered at Kennedy Space Center listened eagerly as the NASA commentator announced the countdown. "T minus forty-five seconds and counting. . . Four. . . three. . .two. . . one – and lift-off!" *Challenger* soared up into the sky. Twenty seconds into lift-off and mission control reported that all engines were running smoothly. Fifty-two seconds in. . . "Challenger go with throttle up," said mission control. "Roger, go with throttle up," said Scobee.

To spectators at Cape Canaveral it seemed that everything was going well. But TV viewers, watching the launch through NASA's telescopic cameras suddenly saw a dull orange glow appear on the belly of the shuttle.

Challenger was on fire. Seventy-three seconds into her mission, the space shuttle *Challenger* exploded. The commentator automatically carried on for a moment and then cut off. After a full minute of silence, his voice came again: "We have a report from the flight dynamics officer that the vehicle has exploded. The flight director confirms that." There was a stunned silence, not only from those actually at Cape Canaveral, but from TV viewers all over America.

Soon after the tragedy, President Reagan appeared on television to address the nation. This was an enormous setback for his space programme, but he rose to the occasion like the old pro he was. The crew of the *Challenger*, he told his audience, had: "Left the surly bonds of earth to touch the face of God." It was hard to understand, he said, why painful things like this had to happen. "It's all part of the process of exploration and expanding man's horizons."

In the days that followed the disaster, NASA, aided by the US Coast Guard, recovered large fragments of the shuttle from the bottom of the Atlantic, including the cabin containing the bodies, which was found intact. The recovered shuttle parts were examined to discover the cause of the explosion. It wasn't too difficult. One of the O-rings, the component about which the rocket engineers had expressed so many doubts, had begun to burn soon after take-off. As a result, the highly-flammable gases in the booster-rocket had ignited. The Senate sub-committee charged with the enquiry into the disaster accused NASA of "a serious flaw in the decision-making process" and called for a major redesign of shuttle technology. It was only after hundreds of improvements to its basic design and to its computer technology, that the next space shuttle *Discovery,* successfully blasted off from Cape Canaveral – thirty-two months later.

The success of the space programme was a symbol of America's strength and the superiority of its technology over that of the Soviet Union. Since the *Challenger* disaster, and the political and social changes Russia has undergone, space has been rather underplayed. Perhaps the glory days of space are already over. Unless of course, one of those UFOs finally lands on the White House lawn . . .

ALSO FROM ROBINSON CHILDREN'S BOOKS

True Mystery Stories   Finn Bevan   **£4.99** { }
Fascinating accounts of the world's strangest phenomena, from ghosts and
water monsters to UFOs and spontaneous human combustion –
really weird!

Space Stories   Ed. Mike Ashley   **£4.99** { }
Over 30 exciting and intriguing space adventures – some take place on a
future Earth, some in our solar system, and some on worlds far away.

Fantasy Stories   Ed. Mike Ashley   **£4.99** { }
Brings together some of the most imaginative fantasy stories this century,
some written especially for this book, others already classics.

Horse Stories   Ed. Felicity Trotman   **£4.99** { }
Wonderful new stories by Monica Edwards, Andrew Lang, and Geraldine
McCaughrean, as well as modern classics by such popular writers as James
Herriot.

Dance Stories   Ed. Felicity Trotman   **£6.99** { }
Exciting, glamorous and romantic stories about the world of dance, from over
thirty top authors.

Robinson Publishing Ltd, PO Box 11, Falmouth, Cornwall TR10 9EN
Tel:+44(0)1326317200 Fax: +44(0)1326317444
Email:books@Barni.avel.co.uk

UK/BFPO customers please allow £1.00 for p&p for the first book, plus 50p
for the second, plus 30p for each additional book up to a maximum charge of
£3.00. Overseas customers (inc Ireland) please allow £2.00 for the first book,
plus £1.00 for the second, plus 50p for each additional book.

Please send me the titles ticked above.

NAME (Block letters) ———————————————————————

ADDRESS ————————————————————————————

————————————————————————————————————

————————————————— POSTCODE ———————————————

I enclose a cheque/PO (payable to Robinson Publishing Ltd) for——————
I wish to pay by Switch/Credit card

————————————————————— Card Expiry Date——————————